GLORY OF AMERICA SERIES!

Willy Finds Victory
A Blessed Francis Seelos Story

By Joan Stromberg
Illustrated by Eileen McCook

BEHOLD PUBLICATIONS
Buckner, KY

Published by

Behold Publications
4503 Mattingly Ct, Suite E
Buckner, KY 40010

502-225-6252
800-884-7649
www.beholdpublications.com

Printed in the United States of America by
St. Martin's Print Shop
3050 Gap Knob Rd.
New Hope, Kentucky 40052

Cover design by: Joseph Stromberg

Many thanks to Fr. Carl Hoegerl, C.S.s.R. for all his help in
researching the life of Blessed Seelos.

To my son Mickey
Our own cheerful saint in progress!

Other books in the Glory of America Series:

The Orphans Find a Home: A St. Frances Cabrini Story

Kat Finds a Friend: A St. Elizabeth Seton Story

Thomas Finds a Treasure: A St. John Neumann Story

ALSO BY JOAN STROMBERG:

The Iron Spy

Table of Contents

Chapter One

MARCH TO FREDERICKSBURG

"Out of the way, boy!" The sound of dozens of rushing horses filled Willy's head like a drumbeat. He whirled around and saw a mass of blue uniforms on brown horses heading right toward him. Whiskers squealed and jumped onto Willy's knapsack as the duo leaped off the road just in time to avoid getting trampled.

The Union Cavalry rushed by at breakneck speed. Willy searched their uniforms and flags as best he could as they whizzed by, trying to find some identifying mark. Could they be from his home state of New York? Or maybe from where he had most recently moved...from Michigan? They were definitely wearing Union blue. Other than that, Willy didn't notice any other distinction in their uniform. If they hadn't been in such a rush, he'd have asked them where they were from and whether they had seen his brother-in-law's regiment, the 24th Michigan.

Willy had seen a lot of soldiers in the last few days, all heading in the same direction. None had seen the 24th Michigan, although they had certainly heard of the famous

Iron Brigade which the 24th Michigan had joined after leaving Detroit the summer before. Most of the soldiers were in too big of a hurry to chat for long with a little boy with a raccoon on his shoulder.

"There's a big one a-brewin'," one thin soldier with a straggly beard had said as he passed Willy earlier that day. "A little tyke like yourself better get back home to your mama." Then the soldier let out a of hoot of laughter.

Little tyke indeed! Willy was nearly ten years old. He was old enough to make it from Michigan to the woods of Virginia all by himself well enough. He even took good care of his pet raccoon, Whiskers, too. He was old enough to go fetch his brother-in-law to come home and help his sister with their new baby who was sick. He even thought he was old enough to help out with the fighting, too, if he were needed. Maybe he'd even take his brother-in-law's place. He was definitely old enough not to run home to his mama, even if he had one.

Whiskers scrambled around the knapsack to rest on the canteen strung across Willy's shoulder. The raccoon's nose twitched as he made little scolding squeaking noises. He clawed his paw at the soldier's backs in a mock challenge.

"You tell them, Whiskers," Willy said. "I agree. They were rude." Whiskers hopped down and began to walk alongside Willy on the edge of the road.

It had been weeks since he left the small town of Trenton on Lake Erie to set out to find his sister's husband. Elizabeth, his sister, had always been delicate and frail. Unlike the rest of the McBlaines, who were of hardy Scottish-Irish stock, Elizabeth was always pale, fragile and beautiful. After she had the baby, a boy named William after his father as well as his uncle, Elizabeth seemed to shrink more every day. The baby wasn't well, either. Elizabeth's husband, Bill Smith, had signed up with the 24th Michigan just days before little Willy was born. But with

Elizabeth's uncle and aunt there to help her, Bill thought that his country needed him more.

Willy didn't see it that way. Each day as his sister grew weaker, Willy grew more desperate. He thought that if she just had her husband returned to her unharmed, she would be alive and beautiful again. Willy planned to bring his brother-in-law home from the war. He'd take his place if he needed to. Besides, who depended on Willy? He didn't have a baby, a wife or even parents to fret over him, so he was the logical choice to take Bill's place.

Willy shivered and pulled his coat tighter around his shoulders as he followed the tracks left by the cavalry. The road headed south, deeper into Virginia, deeper into Rebel territory and further and further from home. The last letter his sister had gotten from her husband was from an encampment near a place called Fredericksburg, Virginia. He knew he had to be close now. It was a good thing, too, because the early December days were getting chilly even in the South. And the December nights were downright cold. He and Whiskers had woken up under a blanket of frost more than once.

He just hoped he wouldn't reach Fredericksburg too late. What if the 24th had left? What if the battle Bill had been waiting for had already happened and Bill was wounded, or worse yet...killed? Willy tried not to think about it as he trudged along through the partially frozen mud. Whiskers had run off into the wood on the side of the road and returned with a paw full of nuts. They came to a bridge over a little creek. Willy decided to fill his canteen. He filled it with clear, cold water and began to break the nuts open against a rock. He heard more tramping feet coming along the road, heading south.

The drummer kept time with the marching feet. "How far to Fredericksburg?" Willy hollered up to him. The drummer glanced at Willy without missing a beat. Willy was

Willy finds the Army of the Potomac

surprised to see a boy about the same age as himself. The boy gave Willy a hard stare, but he didn't answer.

Another soldier, in the long columns behind him, did. "Not far, little fellow. But you don't want to go there. All them folk are evacuating. No bridge either. Leastways, not yet. They say we are going to build a floatin' one cross the Rappahannock River. Won't be much left in Fredericksburg after we get through." Willy saw a yellow-toothed smile underneath the blue forage cap.

"Have you seen anyone from Michigan?" Willy said to the man.

"Nope. We're from Maine. Haven't seen no Michiganders yet."

"All right, cut the chatter," a man with stripes on the shoulders of his blue uniform said. Willy noticed how the men instantly obeyed the man with the long mustaches and sandy-colored hair who led the column of men. He watched as columns of soldiers marched silently to the beat of the drum. He ate his nuts silently as they passed. Even Whiskers ate his nuts without his usual chatter.

After they had passed, Willy got back on the road. It was beginning to get dark now. The woods were thinning out and the road was getting wider as they traveled farther south. Every once in a while, he thought he caught a glimpse of the setting sun bouncing off sparkling water through the trees. He figured it must be the river the soldier had mentioned. He remembered that at the last town he had passed, Warrenton, they had said the army was heading this way, toward the little river town of Fredericksburg. One person had even remembered some Michiganders attached to the Western Iron Brigade there. Their commander had actually been born in the town. Usually, they said, they closed their doors and shutters to the Northern invaders, but word got around that Colonel Morrow, who was born there, had come through with the invading army.

The news that he was so close to his brother-in-law's army sent a chill up Willy's spine and quickened his step. Knowing he was close to the end of his mission drove him harder. He was tired and weary, but he knew he had to reach his brother-in-law before the expected battle.

Suddenly, the woods disappeared altogether and a clearing appeared. Willy gasped. All around him was a sea of white tents set around little campfires twinkling in the twilight. They stretched as far as the eye could see, through a little town, down to the winding waters of a river in the distance. Men sat in all positions around their little fires, some playing cards, others eating, and still others reading or writing on small pieces of paper. Willy stopped dead in his tracks at the sight. Whiskers squeaked and hid his head in the flap on the top of Willy's knapsack. Finally, after traveling by boat, by rail and on foot, Willy had found the Army of the Potomac.

Chapter Two

DISAPPOINTMENT

Slowly, Willy stepped up to the nearest group of tents. They formed a circle around the campfire. Over the fire was a pot with some yellowish water bubbling away in it. A few men in blue were gathered around the fire warming their hands. It was going to be cold again tonight, Willy thought.

A soldier with a scraggly black beard looked up as Willy approached.

"Well, seems we have a visitor, boys," the man said. The other men eyed Willy for a moment, then went back to warming their hands.

"What can we do for you, little fella?" the first man asked.

"I'm looking for a soldier," Willy replied.

"I'd say you found some," the man chuckled.

"It's my brother-in-law," Willy said. "His name is William Smith."

"Smith? Don't know him. Is he from Maine?"

"No, no. We, I mean, he's from Michigan."

"Michigan! You come all the way from Michigan?" the man said, peering more closely at Willy. "Hey, what's that varmint you got on your shoulder?"

Whiskers had peered over Willy's shoulder, afraid of the men, but interested in their dinner.

"It's just my pet raccoon, Whiskers."

"Looks like he's interested in staying for supper," the man said. "He just might make a tasty addition to this stew." The man slapped his knee and let out a hoot of laughter. The other men chuckled under their breath.

Willy shifted his weight from one foot to the other nervously. "Could you tell me if the soldiers from the 24th Michigan are anywhere around?"

"Can't say that I can," the soldier replied. We're Maine men, mostly. You might try down yonder," he pointed toward the river. "Those boys been here longer, waiting on the supplies to build the pontoon bridge. They'd know who was here and who wasn't."

"Much obliged," Willy said. He turned in the direction of the river.

"Sure your raccoon wouldn't want to stay for supper?" the soldier called out to Willy's back. He hooted with laughter again. Willy kept walking, weaving in and out of tents toward the river.

When he had gotten a fair distance from the Maine men, he paused at another campfire. These men wore a very different uniform. Their pants were red and baggy and their jackets had gold with red braid on them. Willy couldn't help thinking that they looked more like they belonged in the circus train he had seen once when they had lived on a canal in New York, rather than on a battlefield. He stepped out of the shadows into the light of their campfire.

"Well, what do we have here?" said a man who was bending over a pot on his fire. "A drummer boy without his drum? You're not in uniform, son."

"No, I'm looking for a soldier from Michigan."

"Not here. We're from New York." The man paused. He gestured to his colorful uniform, "Zouaves." He noticed the questioning look on Willy's face and smiled. "Never seen a Zouave, eh, boy?" Willy shook his head. "We are a sight, all lined up, that's for sure. They say the uniform's from way over there in Europe. Never seen a real European Zouave myself, but we sure can find each other on the battlefield!" Willy smiled. The man was much more friendly than the Maine men he had met a while ago. "Listen here, boy, I don't know where the Michigan fellows are that you're lookin' for. They don't tell us rank and file soldiers what's going on until it's goin' on already! But the captain over there, he would know." The soldier tossed his head in the direction of a larger tent that poked up above the rest. "The officers are over there. C'mon, follow me and we'll find them Michiganders for you."

Willy followed the man toward the large tent. There was a large clearing in front of the tent and several wooden chairs set around a campfire. There was a plank spread across several of the chairs and men gathered around the plank looking at something illuminated by a lantern. The men weren't wearing the colorful uniforms of the soldier. Willy would never have guessed they were from the same company. The New York soldier walked up to a man sitting in a chair reading some papers.

"'Scuse me, sir," the soldier said. The man looked over his shoulder to the soldier.

"Yes, Jenkins?"

"This little fellow over here," the Zouave motioned his head toward Willy, who was trying to hide in the shadows of the lantern, "he's trying to find some Michiganders. You know of a camp 'round here, sir?"

The officer peered past the soldier at Willy. When he turned his head, Willy gasped. Over his left eye, there was a black patch. The firelight and lantern dancing off his face gave him an evil look. Willy sucked in his breath and stood

Jim Jenkins helps Willy find the Iron Brigade

firm. If this was all it took to frighten him, he thought, he didn't deserve to fight in the war in his brother-in-law's place.

"Where you from, boy?" the officer asked.

"Michigan, sir. I'm looking for the 24th Michigan Regiment. Colonel Morrow's troops, sir."

"You come all the way from Michigan, boy?" The officer raised the eyebrow above the patch.

"Yes, sir. It's important I find my sister's husband. She needs to get a message to him." Willy didn't want to reveal to the officer that he meant to send his brother-in-law home and take his place. Some might think his brother-in-law had deserted. Deserters were shot.

"Couldn't she write a letter? Seems a lot safer than sending a boy with a message all the way from Michigan."

Willy shifted his weight from his left foot to his right. "It's a personal message, sir. I have to deliver it personally." Willy looked down at his feet.

"Oh," the captain said and paused. "I see." Willy wondered what he saw. Could he see through Willy's plans to take his brother-in-law's place? "Well, you've come all this way, I suppose sending you five miles farther wouldn't hurt any."

Five miles more! "What do you mean, sir? Is the 24th not here?"

"No, son. They had some sickness up the road on the way from Warrenton. Since we aren't ready to ford the river, they camped up the road at Brandy Station. They got the pneumonia at the first cold spell. One fellow died, I think. They're waiting up there for the pontoon bridge to be built."

Willy's face fell. He still had five miles to go to reach the 24th Michigan! He wouldn't see his brother-in-law today after all.

The officer noticed Willy's disappointment. "Say, Jenkins, you have room in your tent for a traveling Michigander?"

"No problem, sir," the Zouave grinned. Willy smiled. At least he would be warm tonight. "Tomorrow, I'll show you the road to Brandy Station." The soldier put his arm around Willy's shoulder as he led him back to the city of small tents. "Too bad a fellow like you isn't a couple of years older. You're full of determination and spit coming all the way from Michigan by yourself. Could use your kind in a fight. Yes, sir. I bet you wouldn't run from anything them Rebels could throw at you!"

Willy smiled. He was feeling warmer already.

Chapter Three

LEARNING TO PRAY

Willy felt something warm on his ice cold cheeks. He opened one eye and saw only darkness. Slowly, through his sleep, he heard the short shrill notes of the bugle arousing the city of soldiers. The wet warmness returned to his cheeks. Whiskers was licking his face, like he had every morning on their journey. Willy put his arm around his pet and opened the other eye. A faint, gray light was coming through the opening of the tent. As his eyes adjusted to the dim light, Willy could see it had snowed again last night. *They always said the South was warm and sunny,* Willy thought. So far, it had been pretty cold. He was glad for the shelter of the army tent.

He looked around and noticed that the Zouave soldier, who had introduced himself as Jim Jenkins the night before, was already dressed. He was on his knees in the tent with his back to Willy. He knelt perfectly still, except for his hands, which moved slowly over what looked like beads on a chain. Willy had no idea what the man was doing, but something told him he shouldn't ask right now, either. Willy got up and folded up his army blanket.

Jim moved his hands slowly over his forehead and shoulders and turned to smile at Willy.

"Good morning, son," he grinned. "Did you sleep well?"

"Oh, yes, sir."

"Well, we'll have morning roll call and breakfast, and then I can take you to Brandy Station and your brother-in-law."

"Oh, much obliged, sir, but I wouldn't want to impose. Whiskers and I can find our own breakfast and then we'll be off straight away, if you could just point me in the right direction."

Jim let out a hearty laugh. "You are a determined little fellow, aren't you?" He smiled at Willy with a twinkle in his eye. "Look, there's not much for us fellows to do here while we're waiting for those supply folks from Washington to get us the materials for the pontoon bridge. Except, of course, drill, drill and more drill. I could use the stretch and the change of scenery and I'm sure the captain would let me go. So why don't you let me take you to Brandy Station?"

Willy hesitated. He was tempted by Jim's offer. He could use the company and he liked the big, friendly soldier. He had a lot to learn about army life before he took his brother-in-law's place and Jim could help him to learn. Besides, even hardtack and pork, the soldier's rations for breakfast, lunch and dinner, were better than the few nuts Whiskers could hunt up.

"Why, thank you, Mr. Jenkins. I'd like that."

"Please call me Jim. I'm not old enough to be 'Mr. Jenkins.' Gee, I just got these whiskers last year!" Jim let out another laugh, rubbing some soft stubble on his chin. Willy guessed that he was probably only in his late teens.

"Well, we better get moving, if we're going to make Brandy Station this morning."

On the road to Brandy Station, Jim talked about the last battle he had fought. "All the fellows back at camp already know all the stories. It's good to have a fresh ear," he said. He talked about meeting General Lee's troops in a field near a creek called Antietam. "Can you imagine that Reb General Lee thought he could invade the North?" Jim said. "Well, the fighting was hot. Never seen it any hotter. We walked shoulder to shoulder right at the Reb's fire. I never prayed so hard in my life. I swear I could just feel my guardian angel protecting me like a shield. The fellow on my left shoulder fell, then the feller on my right shoulder and all the time I was just a-praying." Willy's eyes were wide as they walked along the snow-covered road. Whiskers was standing perfectly still on Willy's shoulder as if he, too were listening to the tale of the battle. Jim pulled out his army canteen and took a long drink.

"What happened next?" Willy said impatiently.

"Well, we reached this stone wall and crouched down for cover. Then I loaded and shot, loaded and shot over and over again. I couldn't see no Rebs. All I saw was smoke. Smoke and more smoke. I didn't hear no Rebel yell, either. All I heard was cannon and rifle fire. All of a sudden, the Cap yells 'Forward, charge!' and I look back to see a whole 'nother regiment of our men in blue coming up behind us. We went over the wall and found the Rebels. I got close enough to see them then. They turned and ran like scared kittens. I felt so good at that point, I think I could have chased the whole lot of them straight back to Richmond." Jim paused to let his story sink in.

"I read about that battle in Maryland," Willy said. "They say the North won, but could have licked Lee altogether and ended the war."

"Yep. Generals are men, though, just like soldiers. Sometimes they don't know what to do. Now we're facing

General Lee again." Jim looked over his shoulder at the river growing smaller as they walked away from it. "Lee's right over that river on the other side of town in those high grounds beyond. He'll wait there all winter if he has to. He won't have to, though. They say that as soon as the bridge is built, we're crossing the Rappahannock and driving Lee out of Virginny, too."

"Wow." Willy let it sink in that he just might be able to fight in the next big battle. "Can't you wait?" he asked Jim anxiously.

Jim stopped in his tracks and looked at Willy seriously. "I grew up a lot at Antietam. War is not all glory and victory. It is death and struggle and bravery and cowardice. You see God and the devil and yourself as you truly are, in all your ugliness, on the battlefield. I pray every day I'll never have to see it again. But I also pray that if I do, as my duty requires, I'll do it with courage." Jim began slowly walking again. Willy was confused. He had never heard a battle described as Jim had just said it was. He didn't know what he meant. Still, he wanted to hear more about Antietam.

"Did you kill any Rebs, Jim?"

Jim paused for a moment and then answered in almost a whisper. "Yes."

Something in Jim's voice made Willy realize that he didn't want to talk about it anymore. An uncomfortable silence followed.

"Say, your guardian angel must be working over-time," Jim said cheerfully, patting Willy on the back. "Got to have a good guardian angel to keep you safe all the way from Michigan by yourself."

"I'm not by myself," Willy replied. "I've got Whiskers here. You could say he's my guardian angel." Willy wasn't sure what a guardian angel was, exactly.

"Oh, pets are good, but not nearly as good as a guardian angel," Jim said.

"But Whiskers warns me of danger, wakes me up each morning, helps find food for both us and keeps me company."

"Sounds like a right good friend, all right," Jim nodded. After a pause, he added, "But only your guardian angel could help you in real danger, like mine did at Antietam."

Willy was wide-eyed. "Did you actually see your angel?"

"Well, no," Jim admitted. "But I knew he was there just as sure as you know Whiskers is on your shoulder. I could feel him, you know?"

Willy didn't know, but he was too polite to question an elder, even if it was only a teen-aged soldier. Somehow, Jim acted older than his years.

"Haven't you ever prayed and felt a peaceful feeling, like a warm hug?" Jim asked.

Willy shook his head. "Can't say I ever prayed much."

"What!" Jim stopped dead in his tracks on the road. "How could you never have prayed? Everybody has done it sometimes. Didn't your parents ever teach you?"

"My parents died when I was young in a cholera epidemic along the Erie Canal. My sister and I went to live with my dad's brother. Uncle John doesn't abide religion much. He says it's the waste of fools."

Jim was shaking his head slowly as he began walking again. "Couldn't be more wrong," he said quietly. "I think your uncle would think differently if he ever heard those Rebel bullets whizzing past his ears. I bet then, he couldn't get enough of praying!" Jim chuckled.

"Could you teach me how to pray?" Willy asked.

"Sure, ain't nothin' to it. First you start out by saying, 'Hello, God, how are you?' by saying 'In the name of the Father, and of the Son, and of the Holy Ghost.'" Jim put his hand on his forehead when he said "Father," on his chest

Jim Jenkins shows Willy how to pray

when he said "Son," and on his shoulders when he said "Holy" and "Ghost."

Willy imitated him. "I saw you doing that this morning. You had something in your hand, too."

"Oh, that's my Rosary," Jim said as he brought forth a string of beads from his pocket. Willy thought he had never seen anything more beautiful. The glass beads glistened and danced with light like a new-fallen snow.

"How does it work? Can you teach me to say those prayers?"

Jim laughed at his eagerness.

"For each of the beads, you say a prayer," he began.

"Each one?" Willy was wide-eyed. "That's a lot of prayin'!"

Jim let out his hearty laugh again. "We'll start with something a little more simple, I think. Mmmm, how about we start out with the 'Prayer to the Guardian Angel,' Repeat it after me: Angel of God..."

"Angel of God," Willy began slowly, trying to impress each word into his memory.

"My guardian dear..."

"My guardian dear..."

"To whom God's love commits me here..."

"To whom God's love commits me here..."

"Ever this day be at my side..."

"Ever this day be at my side..."

"To light, to guard, to rule, to guide..."

"To light, to guard, to rule, to," Willy hesitated, thinking hard, "to guide."

"Perfect!" Jim exclaimed. "Now you try it by yourself." Willy said the prayer slowly, needing help from Jim with only the last part. "You're a fast learner, boy." Willy grinned at Jim's praise. "You're going to be able to learn the Rosary in no time. But you're going to have to ask a priest or someone else to teach you, because look up ahead, boy."

Willy looked down the road and saw the now-familiar sight of a city of white triangles in a clearing. Soldiers were camped in the field. They had reached Brandy Station.

Chapter Four

DANGER ON THE ROAD

"What's the name again?" The man with the spectacles sat behind the table with a book in front of him.

"Smith, William Smith, of Company B," Willy said. There were nearly a thousand men in his brother-in-law's regiment and there were several more regiments camped nearby. Jim said going straight to the regimental headquarters would save time finding his brother-in-law.

"Smith, Smith, ahh, here it is." The man moved his finger down the column of writing, stopped and looked up. "Sent down to Fortress Monroe on disability."

Willy felt like someone had punched him in the stomach. "What!" he said in disbelief. "He's not here? Are you sure?"

"Says right here." The man turned the book so Willy could read it. "William Smith, 24th Michigan, Company B, disability, Fortress Monroe Hospital, December 5." Willy read the entry, blinked and read it again. Jim put his hand on Willy's shoulder.

"Yeah, had a lot of sickness here," the man in the spectacles said. "Pneumonia something fierce. This William Smith no doubt took ill and they sent him on the boat heading for the Fort. Good hospital there. He'll be taken care of, sonny, don't worry."

Willy only half heard what the man was saying. How could he have finally reached the 24th Michigan and his brother-in-law not be here? It was his worst fear being realized.

"Where is this Fortress Monroe?" Willy asked.

"Why, it's way down at the mouth of the Chesapeake Bay," the man answered. "Down near Hampton Roads."

"How do I get there? Which road is Hampton Road?" Willy looked around to find his options.

The man laughed. "Hampton Roads is where the James River meets the Chesapeake. Can't get there by any road. Not safe to go that far into Reb territory. Safest way is by boat. You're not fixin' on going, are you, lad?" The man asked.

"I have to," Willy replied, looking from Jim's concerned face to the face of the man with the glasses. "I've come this far and I have to get to my brother-in-law, no matter what."

The man with the glasses just shook his head. "Determined little fellow, isn't he?" he said to Jim.

Jim nodded. "Look, Willy, I know how much this means to you, but I don't think going further south is safe at all. Your family must be worried. Let me send you on a train back to Michigan."

Willy set his jaw firmly. "I've come this far and I'm not going back without seeing my brother-in-law and delivering my message." Jim looked at the man and shrugged. Willy knew that they couldn't say anything to change his mind.

"Well, you'll have that overworked guardian angel with you," Jim said, smiling. "You've made it this far and I'm sure you'll make it the rest of the way." He looked at the man still holding the regimental books. "Do you have a couple of extra rations for this soldier on a mission?" The man looked from Willy to Jim and nodded.

"I suppose we have a few to spare." He got up from his chair. "Wait right here and I'll get some supplies."

"Well, Willy," Jim said after the man had gone, "looks like your journey's not over yet. You just keep asking your guardian angel for help and you'll be fine." Jim reached into his pocket and pulled out his chain of beads. He looked at their beauty shining in the sunlight in the palm of his hand. Slowly, he closed his hand and reached out and dropped the beads into Willy's hand. "Here, you may need these more than I do."

"But, Jim, it's so beautiful! You don't want to part with it! I couldn't take it." Willy tried to hand the Rosary back to Jim.

"No, no, you need it more than I do right now. I'll write home and ask them to send me another one. Maybe the priest back at camp has a spare. Either way, I still have my fingers to use when saying my prayers." Jim smiled the saddest, kindest smile Willy had ever seen.

"But Jim, I don't even know how to pray the Rosary," Willy protested again.

"It doesn't matter. You'll learn. Find a priest and he'll show you." Jim paused. "I'm sorry I can't go with you to Fortress Monroe. Write me when you can...54th New York, Duryee's Zouaves; Company K. Don't forget!"

"I won't forget, Jim." Willy said. How could he? He'd never had a virtual stranger been as nice to him as Jim had been. Willy looked down at the sparkling beads in his hand. They were so beautiful! He slipped them in his pocket. He put his arms around Jim's waist. All the way from Michigan, through the long cold nights and exhausting days, Willy had never cried. Now, he wanted to cry.

It was late afternoon and Willy was still on the road to the landing where he could catch a boat to Fortress Monroe. His hand was in his pocket fingering the Rosary Jim had given him. His mind wandered to thoughts of his brother-in-law lying in the hospital. What would he do when he found him? Would he nurse him back to health so he could return to his sister and her baby in Michigan? He didn't know anything about curing sick people. If he had, he wouldn't have left his sister in the first place. All he knew was that he had to tell his brother-in-law that his sister and the baby needed him. When his brother-in-law was well enough, he had to send him home. Then he'd hurry back to Fredericksburg before the fight. He'd fight alongside Jim Jenkins and their guardian angels would make them invincible!

Suddenly, a shot rang out and a bullet whizzed past Willy's ear. Whiskers screeched, jumped off Willy's shoulder and scuttled under a log next to the road. Instinctively, Willy ducked and jumped behind the log, too. It wasn't much of a hiding place. The trees were bare and the leaves were crisp and crunchy underfoot. Willy felt strong hands on his overcoat lifting him up. They lifted him so high, his feet were no longer touching the ground. The hands turned him around until he was face to face with a crooked nose, yellow teeth, a graying beard and a mouth full of foul breath. Willy gasped and tried to remember the words of the angel prayer Jim had taught him, but he was too scared.

"Look what we caught here, Amos," the man with the foul breath said. For the first time, Willy looked at their uniforms. His eyes opened wide. Their uniforms were dyed butternut...the color of the enemy...the color of the South. The man from the 24th had warned him that there would be scouts along the road to the boat landing. Willy wished he had been paying better attention rather than letting his mind wander on his worries.

"Got anything of value, boy?" The man with the foul breath peered at Willy.

"C'mon Harvey, let the boy go. We're supposed to be scoutin', not foragin'," the other Reb said.

"We can do both, can't we?" the first man said. He let Willy's feet touch the ground but didn't let up on his hold. "Whachya got in that knapsack, little fella? Got any coffee? Do anythin' for some good Yankee coffee."

"Yes," Willy said as he spotted a way of escape. "If you let me go, I'll give you all my coffee." He knew the sergeant for the 24th had included coffee in his rations. He wasn't overly fond of the coffee, so he was more than willing to give it up for his freedom. The men could take his food. He'd be able to get some more somehow. But he didn't want them to find Jim's Rosary...his Rosary. To him, Jim's gift was more precious than food.

The Reb with the foul breath took off Willy's knapsack and began to rummage through it. He pulled out the package of coffee beans. "What else you got in here?"

"Just get the coffee and let's get back across river," the other Reb said. He was nervously looking up and down the road. He held his rifle tightly in both hands. "C'mon, Harvey, c'mon. I think I hear somebody comin.'"

"Hold your horses, Amos. Let me see what else is in this here knapsack. What's this?" he pulled out another package stamped "U.S.A." "Army rations?" The man looked at Willy suspiciously. "You a spy, boy?" Willy shook his head.

"Harvey, c'mon, he's just a boy. Grab the stuff and let's go."

Harvey ignored his friend again. "Are you a spy, boy?" he said again.

"No," Willy stammered. "No, sir." How did that prayer go? Willy tried hard to remember. *Angel of God, my guardian dear...*

Willy is caught by Rebel scouts!

"You're one of them, though. Can tell by that north-ern Yankee accent you got, boy."

"Oh, let him go, Harvey. Just let him go. We're on their side of the river, remember?"

Harvey shot his fellow soldier an evil look. "Virginny's ours, not theirs. They'se the invaders. Don't ever forget that, Amos."

"All right, all right, Harvey. It's ours. Don't get a coon up your britches."

Harvey turned his attention back toward Willy. "Where'd you get these army rations, boy?"

"Just up the road a bit," Willy managed to say through chattering teeth. The cold seemed to sink to his bones since the Rebs nabbed him. *To whom God's love commits me here...*

"Up the road? How many Yanks are up the road? How many regiments? What's the number of soldiers?"

"I don't know, sir," Willy answered. The man began to shake Willy. The fist holding Willy's overcoat was nearly as big as Willy's whole head. The man was strong, too. Willy's teeth chattered harder. *Ever this day be at my side...*

"Shhh," Amos said, holding his rifle perfectly still. "Did you hear that?"

Harvey stopped shaking Willy and the trio stood still.

"I don't hear nothin'," Harvey said. "You're jitterier than a scaird possum."

Just then, there was a faint rustling of leaves. "There it is again," Amos said. The rustling got louder and closer. The men peered through the bare trees on either side of the road.

"Prob'ly some varmint out for a stroll in the woods," Harvey said.

"Well, I'm not waiting to find out," Amos replied. "Just let the boy go and let's get out of here. This here road is too wide open. We gotta find some cover." Amos began running for the denser forest before Harvey could respond.

Before Willy knew it, Harvey had let him go and was following Amos through the forest, stuffing his newly-acquired package of coffee into his butternut-colored uniform. In a moment, they were out of sight. *To light, to guard, to rule and guide...*

Willy let out a sigh of relief. The leaves rustled behind him off the side of the road. He held his breath and turned slowly as the sound grew. Was it another soldier? Was this one a Yank or a Reb? Could it be a bear or some other hungry animal looking for an early winter meal? As he turned, a mound of fur leaped toward his head and landed on his shoulder.

"Whiskers! It was you all along! Thanks, pal."

Chapter Five

MEETING FATHER SEELOS

The wharf was bustling with activity. Boats of every size and shape lined the waters of the Potomac River at Aquia Creek Landing. Whiskers ducked back into Willy's knapsack, as he always did when the noise and crowd of Willy's travels were too much for him.

Union soldiers were everywhere. Some were loading and unloading the boats; others leaned against the dock piers smoking or talking. Around one post, a group of boys not much older than Willy were piling up crates marked: US Army Danger: Explosives. The boys were dressed in blue, but in a uniform Willy had never seen before. Their pants were long and baggy and their blue baggy shirts had large collars with white piping. On their heads they wore a flat-top cap with a tail hanging down the back. Willy approached the boys.

"Excuse me," he said, but the boys didn't break the rhythm of their work. One glanced at Willy, but didn't stop. "Can you tell me if any of these boats are going to Fortress Monroe?"

"Yeah," one fellow lugging a crate said. "My ship, *The Lady Jane,* is due at Fortress Monroe with this gunpowder tomorrow."

"Great!" Willy said. "Can I go with you?"

"My captain doesn't like passengers," the lad said. Willy's face must have shown his disappointment. The boy stopped and looked at Willy. "Why are you so hot to get to Fortress Monroe?"

"I have a close relative in the hospital there. I *have* to see him. It's urgent. I've come all the way from Michigan."

"Michigan! By yourself?" The other boys stopped their work for a moment and looked at Willy. There was a little more respect in their eyes.

"Yes. Well, my pet raccoon came with me," Willy said. Whiskers peeked his bandit eyes out of the knapsack when Willy mentioned him.

The boy with the crate set it down and came over to pet Whiskers. "Oh, I have a pet raccoon back home, too. What's his name?"

"Whiskers."

"If I get you aboard the *Lady Jane*, can I play with him?" the lad said as if he were ten years old again instead of a soldier in the Union Navy.

"Yeah, sure," Willy agreed readily.

"Meet me here in an hour, when it's dark, and I'll get you aboard the *Lady Jane.* By the way, my name is Frank. Frank Murphy."

"Willy McBlaine." The boys shook hands.

An hour later, Willy and Whiskers were waiting by the dock when Frank came up silently behind them. Frank was short and stocky and it was hard to tell if he was thirteen years old or eighteen. Willy imagined him on the young side since he wanted to convince himself that he was not too young to take his brother-in-law's place in the army. If Frank could be a soldier, so could Willy.

"Psst," Frank said nearly at Willy's ear, making him jump and Whiskers squeak. "Quiet! I'll have to sneak you on board and put you in my bunk. Since it's just turned dark, the deck sentry is still at supper. We have to go quickly."

Willy crouched down like Frank and followed him toward the boat. They went up the plank, keeping low and in the shadows. Just as they reached the deck of the boat, the sentry appeared on deck. Frank ducked in the shadow of the lifeboat on deck and Willy followed. Frank motioned for Willy to follow him below deck. Frank's bunk was a narrow board hanging from the ceiling of the deck. There were three other bunks with men lounging in them in his compartment.

"Don't worry about my mates," Frank said. "They won't say anything about bringing a stowaway aboard. Not unless you're a Reb?"

"Oh, I'm no Reb," Willy assured them. The other men nodded.

"Can I see that raccoon now?" Frank said. Willy took his knapsack off and opened it up. Whiskers cautiously came out.

"It's okay, Whiskers, these are our friends."

Frank began to make a clicking sound with his mouth that sounded just like a raccoon call. Whisker's ears perked up and a confused look came across his masked eyes. He heard another 'coon, but couldn't see one. He seemed to finally figure out that it was Frank making the noise and came right to him.

"He likes me!" Frank said.

"I think you speak his language," Willy said. The boys laughed.

"Can I sleep with him tonight? I miss my 'coon so bad. He'll make me think of home." Frank's eyes pleaded.

"Sure. Where are you from?" Willy asked.

"Maine. We came a long way, too. But we took the water route."

"Have you been in the navy long?"

"Just joined up this summer. I thought it would be adventurous. Mostly it's boring." The other men listening nodded.

"At least they let you enlist. People keep telling me I'm too young."

"Well, they have powder monkeys as young as you in the navy," Frank said.

"Powder monkeys? What's that?"

"I'm a powder monkey. I load the powder in the guns when there's a battle. Haven't done it yet, though. Mostly, we just move supplies from here to there. And drill. Drill. Drill. Drill." Frank nuzzled his nose into Whiskers' fur. "Oh, he smells like the woods. I miss the woods."

"Better get some rest, boys. We'll be in Hampton Roads in the morning," one of the men lying on the bunks said. Willy and Frank were small enough to share Frank's bunk. They curled up and were soon fast asleep.

Willy woke up to Whisker's wet tongue on his cheek. He smiled before he opened his eyes, expecting to find himself under the trees and morning skies where he had often spent his nights since leaving home. Instead, the gray dark interior of the boat greeted his eyes. In the dim light, he could make out the sailors dressing quietly. He felt the boat moving through the water.

"How long have we been moving?" Willy asked.

"Since before dawn. It won't be long before we're at Fortress Monroe. When we get there, you stay here until we unload the cargo. I have to go up on deck and help with the docking," Frank said as he tucked his shirt into his pants. "Then you can sneak out with the crates. Do you have anything to eat for breakfast?"

"Yes, I have some rations in my knapsack. Thanks for everything, Frank."

"Good luck, Willy." The boys shook hands. Frank reached out and touched the top of Whiskers' head. Willy noticed the soft, far-away look in Frank's eyes. He didn't look much like a sailor anymore.

After they docked, Willy and Whiskers had no trouble following the crates off the boat. The first thing Willy noticed when he stepped out onto the dock was the scent of the salt water and the sea all around him. Fortress Monroe seemed to be on a piece of land sticking way out into the bay. It was almost completely surrounded by water. Across one of the inlets, Willy noticed a town. Frank told him that it was called Hampton. "The Rebs abandoned it pretty much since it's so close to the Fort." Frank pointed to the ships out in the bay. He said some were U.S. Navy ships preventing any Reb ships from coming into the sea. "Some of them always think they can get by us, though," Frank said. "Then they get the guns from the Fort aimed at them. They haven't got a chance."

Willy helped Frank unload the crates as they talked. Frank had been to Fortress Monroe before, so he told Willy where to find the hospital building where his brother-in-law would be. As much as Willy wanted to get there as soon as possible, he felt he owed it to Frank to help him in his work.

"You're a pretty good hand for such a small guy," Frank said. "Ever think of signing up on a ship? Have you had any experience on a ship before?"

"Well, my brother-in-law, the one in the hospital here, was a ferryman on Lake Erie. I'd help him when he needed it. I learned to handle a small craft. Lake Erie looks a lot like this bay. But the smell is different."

"It's the salt water. Is this the first time you've seen the ocean?"

"Yes. It's magnificent!"

The boys finished their work and said their good-byes. Willy wondered whether he'd ever see Frank again, or whether Frank would ever meet the exciting battle he was looking for.

Willy found the hospital without a problem, thanks to Frank's directions. There were wounded men standing around smoking cigarettes outside the door. Some were leaning on crutches with the bottom portion of their leg missing and bandaged, some were missing arms or fingers, and others just looked tired.

A nurse was sitting at a desk with charts and papers scattered on it when Willy entered the building. She shuddered as the cold December wind came in with Willy. "Close the door, please!"

Willy closed the door and went over to the desk. "I'm looking for my brother-in-law. His regiment said he was brought here last week with pneumonia. His name is William Smith."

"If he was brought here with pneumonia, it must be pretty bad," the nurse said. "Last week, you said? Do you know what day?"

"I'm not sure. Oh, I remember. The sergeant said it was December 5th."

"Smith, you said? That's a common enough name. What regiment?" She was searching the files in front of her.

"24th Michigan, ma'am," Willy answered.

"Smith, Smith, Smith," the woman said to herself. "Oh, here it is. William Smith, 24th Michigan, pneumonia. Looks like he's due for a discharge on disability. Seems he's had a pretty hard time of it."

"What does that mean?" Willy said.

Father Seelos walks with Willy through the hospital

"They're sending him home. He's not fit to fight."

"Sending him home?" Willy couldn't believe his ears. He had come all this way to take his brother-in-law's place in the fight and they were sending him home!

"Oh, hello, Father," the nurse said as the door opened again and a tall man with glasses and a pleasant smile came through. He wore a long black garment with a black overcoat and a four-cornered hat with a kind of point in the center. After nodding to the nurse, he stood behind Willy until the boy's business with the nurse was finished.

"William Smith is in Ward F, toward the left there, bed 33." The nurse pointed down a corridor in front of the desk. The nurse's attention then turned to the man in black. Willy stood for a moment, partly out of curiosity about the new visitor and partly because it was still sinking in that his trip was nearly over and had been fruitless from the beginning.

"What can I do for you, Father?" the nurse asked. Willy thought the man must be a priest. He thought of the Rosary Jim had given him. He reached in his pocket and fingered the beads. This priest would be able to tell him how to pray the Rosary.

"I'm just here to visit the men, nurse," the priest said. Willy waited to see if he was going the same way Willy was going. The priest turned toward Willy. "Do you have someone here who may need to see a priest?" Willy had never seen a kinder face. He knew right away that this priest was someone he could trust.

"I'm just here to see my brother-in-law," Willy began.

"Well, let's go see him together." The priest put his arm around Willy's shoulder as they headed toward Ward F. "I'm Father Seelos. What's your name?"

"Willy. Willy McBlaine."

"Nice to meet you, Willy McBlaine."

When they went through the doors to the wards, the smell of sickness nearly knocked Willy off his feet. Father Seelos just continued to smile. The men filled the rows of beds, some sitting and talking, others lying down, sleeping, and others rolling slightly in their pain. Some of them called out to the priest. He waved and promised to return shortly. "I'll get to them on the way out. Ward F is pretty far down the corridor." Willy was glad for Father Seelos' arm around his shoulder. He was slowly getting used to the smell, but he wasn't sure how he would have made it without the priest's support.

Finally they made it to Ward F. The nurse on the Ward pointed to bed 33. "Does he know you are coming?" Father Seelos asked Willy, sensing his nervousness.

"No." Willy was nervous. He wasn't sure whether his brother-in-law would be pleased or upset with him for coming all this way by himself.

They approached the man on the bed, who was facing away from them. They couldn't tell whether he was asleep or awake.

"Bill?" Willy said gently. "Bill Smith?" The man turned slowly and faced the priest and the boy.

"Yes?" the man said weakly.

There must be some mistake! This wasn't Willy's brother-in-law! Who was this man?

Chapter Six

MISTAKEN IDENTITY

"**A**re you Bill Smith?" Father Seelos sensed there was something not right.

"Well, sometimes my mama calls me Billy, but not since I was a youngster," the man said.

"But you are William Smith?" Father Seelos asked.

"That's me. Most people call me Will."

"But you're not related to this young man?" Father Seelos motioned toward Willy.

The man narrowed his eyes and looked at Willy. "No, can't say I've ever seen the lad before."

"You—you're William Smith from Michigan?" Willy stammered.

"Yep. Say, what's this all about?"

"The 24th Michigan? Company B?" Willy asked.

"Yep, that's me. This pneumonia hit me hard, but I still know who I am." Suddenly, a light came across William Smith's face. "Oh, you must be looking for Bill Smith. One of the Trenton Boys. The ferryman."

"Yes," Willy said.

The man waved his hand back and forth in front of his face. "There were two of us. I'm William Smith from Detroit. They called me 'William Smith the first' and the Trenton William Smith, 'William Smith the second.' I guess you didn't tell them which one you were looking for, did you?"

"No," Willy said feebly. "I didn't know there were two."

"'Course not. How could you? Did they send you all the way from Brandy Station?"

"Actually, I came all the way from Michigan." Willy felt this huge lump inside, like he couldn't believe what he was hearing. Here he was, finally at the end of the journey, and the man he came to see wasn't his brother-in-law!

"All the way from Michigan?" Father Seelos and Will Smith said together. "On your own?" Father Seelos added.

Willy nodded. He felt tears coming up from the lump in his stomach. He didn't want to cry in front of all these strangers. He was glad for Father Seelos' arm around his shoulders. He felt like the strong arm was keeping his insides from spilling out.

"Sorry about that, son," Will Smith said. "But as far as I know, your Bill Smith is back with the army getting ready to fight a big one, from what I hear."

Willy turned and started slowly moving down the corridor. He didn't see, hear or smell anything now. He felt numb all over. Even the lump in his stomach felt numb. What was he supposed to do now? Go back to Fredericksburg? The expected battle was supposed to happen any day. What if he missed it and his brother-in-law was killed in the battle and was never coming home? Willy never would forgive himself for making such a stupid mistake.

"How about a cup of tea?" Willy was so absorbed in his own thoughts that he hadn't realized that Father Seelos was still walking through the wards with his arm around Willy's shoulder. The priest's voice was kind and gentle.

"Thanks for everything, sir — er, Father," Willy said quietly, "but I better get on the boat back to Aquia Creek Landing before it leaves the dock."

"Willy," Father Seelos stopped and looked at Willy gently but firmly. "Won't you come and sit with me and let's take some time to figure out what to do."

Willy hesitated, "But Father, you have to see all these other men, too. They are much more important than I am."

Father Seelos smiled. "There is no one in the world as important as you, Willy."

Willy returned the smile. The numbness inside began to wear off. He absently put his hand in his pocket and felt the string of beads Jim had given to him. Jim had told him a priest would be able to teach him better how to pray. Perhaps, with the help of this priest, Willy could get rid of the rest of the numbness and know for certain what was the best thing to do. He nodded to Father Seelos as they walked out of the hospital together.

"You are one brave young man," Father Seelos said after Willy finished telling his adventurous tale. Willy smiled. He liked Father Seelos. He was the first grown-up who hadn't told him he should give up his quest and just go home. "Very brave, indeed," Father Seelos repeated. "I can see why you were so disappointed at finding that the man in the hospital was not your brother-in-law. What will you do now?"

Father Seelos treated Willy like an equal. He didn't talk down to Willy, but as if Willy could make his own decisions and they just might be the right ones.

"I'm going back to Fredericksburg."

Father Seelos grinned. "I expected that." Again, Willy was surprised that Father didn't talk him out of his determination. "Can I ask a favor before you go, Willy? In exchange for the tea, maybe?"

"What is it?"

"I'm giving a talk to the men in the hospital in a few minutes. Would you delay going back to Fredericksburg until after the talk? Then, at least, I can give you a proper goodbye and a blessing."

Willy shrugged his shoulders, "Sure, Father. That reminds me," Willy reached into his pocket and pulled out the pearly beads that Jim had given him. "Can you show me how to pray on these?"

Father took the Rosary in his hands and examined it. "It is beautiful, Willy. I didn't know you were Catholic."

"Oh, I'm not. It's from a soldier I met in Fredericksburg. He told me that I should pray more and he gave me that. He didn't have time to tell me how to pray it, but he did tell me that if I came across a priest, he'd be able to tell me."

"Well, your friend was right. Everyone needs to pray. Especially when things in life get tough. If you stick around for my talk, I'll tell you how to pray the Rosary." The priest grinned at the boy. Willy smiled back.

Father Seelos walked into the hospital's common room where the men able to leave their beds were gathered. Willy slipped into the rear of the room as Father stood behind the table covered with a white cloth. On the table stood a cross with the figure of Christ on it and two lit candles.

"In the name of the Father and of the Son and of the Holy Ghost." Father made the same motions that Jim had taught Willy when beginning to pray. The men followed the priest's example. Willy did, too.

"Men, have faith. God is there, a good, loving, kind God, who sends His angels and His saints to watch over you. He will never abandon you. He is always faithful. Whether you are here, recovering in the hospital at Fortress Monroe, at home with your loved ones, or on some distant battlefield, He will not abandon you.

"Have hope. Because God loves you, He will do what is best for you. Have hope that no matter what happens, it is because He loves you and wants you to be with Him in heaven after your time on earth is through.

"Most of all have love. Love your brothers. Love the man in the next bed, in the next tent and even in the next army. Yes, Jesus tells us to love our enemies. Even those men in the Confederate Army. We are to love them, also." Father Seelos paused as a murmur went through the crowd of men. Willy felt the uncomfortable tension in the room. "We are to love the men, simply because they are men, made in the image and likeness of God. They may be your enemy, but we must love them with the love of Christ. You may be commanded to fight them, even commanded to kill them, but you don't have to hate them to do your duty." The room grew quiet as the men thought about what the priest was saying.

"As Catholic Christian men, you can do this," Father Seelos said. "You have been given a grace by God to love your enemy. You have been given the grace to survive the rigors of army life to come to this point. Think of your poor comrades on the field of battle who did not have the opportunity to make peace with God before their end. You have been given a great grace to want to come to Him, the loving Father, through the Sacraments. Every man on those battlefields, whether fighting for the North or the South, has to face his Maker. We love our fellow soldier because our Heavenly Father loves the fellow soldier, whether he is wearing a blue uniform or a gray one.

"Oh, you sinners who have not courage to confess your sins because they are so numerous or so grievous or so shameful! O, come without fear or trembling! I promise to receive you with all mildness. If I do not keep my word, I here publicly give you permission to cast it up to me in the confessional and to charge me with a falsehood." Father Seelos paused and the men nodded their heads in admiration for his words.

"Serve God through service to one another. Love God through love of one another. Then you will truly be a peace in the middle of a war."

Willy looked down at his hands to think about what the priest had said. He had never heard any other man talk about loving the Rebels. He only thought of beating them. He heard a sniffle from a man next to him. A tear ran down the man's cheek and glistened in the afternoon sunlight streaming through the windows. When Willy looked around, he noticed that many of the men were moved to tears. Several had gathered around Father Seelos and were shaking his hand.

"God bless you, Father."

"You have lifted my heart."

"Thanks so much for coming, Father."

"Father, do you have time to hear my Confession?"

Father Seelos shook each man's hand and gave him the same kindly smile that had put Willy at ease the first time he met the priest.

"Men, I will be hearing Confessions in the chapel for as long as you need me. Please feel free to come by for a visit."

Willy ran to catch up with the priest as he headed out the door.

"Father, can I come with you?"

"Oh, of course, Willy. I promised to teach you the Rosary, didn't I? Well, come to the church with me and I'll

Father Seelos hands a Bible to Willy

give you a copy of the prayer called the *Hail Mary,* and you can memorize it while I hear these men's Confessions."

"What's 'Confession'?" Willy asked.

Father Seelos laughed. "Oh, Willy, it is a great gift of Christ to His Church. Come, walk with me and I'll tell you." The boy and the priest bundled up before heading out into the biting wind to make their way to the chapel.

"Brrr. It is a cold one. The weather in your America changes so quickly. It's a wonder the hospital's aren't all full of patients with pneumonia!"

"Where are you from, Father?"

"Germany. I have been here for many, many years, though."

"Do you miss your family?"

"Yes, very much," answered the priest. "Do you miss yours, Willy?" Father gave him a sideways glance.

"Yes. But I had to come here. My sister is sick and she had a baby right after my brother-in-law went off to war. He has to go back home to her. He just has to. I have to convince him that I can take his place in the army so that my sister will have her husband back."

"I see," Father Seelos said.

"I know I can fight, Father. I'm stronger than I look and I don't mind taking orders. There is only one thing that's bothering me."

"What's that, Willy?"

"What you said in there...about loving our enemy. How can I love someone I'm supposed to kill?"

Father Seelos sighed. "It is one of the most awful things about a war. Some people never can do it. Others love killing those they are supposed to love. Make sure, Willy, that if you do join this war, you never love killing. Do your duty, but remember that they are men, too."

Again, Willy was surprised that Father Seelos didn't try to talk him out of his desire to be a soldier in his brother-in-law's place.

"So, Father, tell me about Confession."

"Christ gave His Church the seven Sacraments to help us to receive the graces we need to be with Him forever in heaven. Confession is where a sinner tells his sins through the priest to God and God gives the sinner absolution through the priest. It is very simple and direct means of cleansing the soul."

Willy wasn't sure he understood it fully. He hadn't really thought of his sins before. They had reached the door of the church. *Our Lady, Star of the Sea,* read the sign out front. The small stone church seemed to welcome him and he went inside following Father Seelos. Father Seelos took a card from his pocket and gave it to Willy.

"Here is a holy card with the *Hail Mary* printed on the back. Let me see your Rosary again." Willy pulled the beads from his pocket. "On these five sets of ten beads, you say this prayer," Father said, first pointing to the beads and then to the holy card. "Do you know the *Our Father?*" Father Seelos asked. Willy slowly shook his head. Father reached over and took a book from one of the benches in rows throughout the church. "Matthew 6:10-13," he said, flipping pages. "Here it is. Now on the large beads, you say this prayer from the Bible. Know these prayers and you will know most of the Rosary."

The men from the hospital began to filter into the church. Father left Willy standing in the back of the church as he disappeared through a door near the entrance. The men began to file in silently and line up next to the door along the wall. Willy took his book, holy card and Rosary and sat in a pew to pray. He felt a quiet peace in his heart as he looked up at the altar with the single red candle burning, the men shuffling their feet quietly at the back of the church, and his Rosary beads in his hands. The words on the page came easily now. He wished he could feel this peaceful always.

Chapter Seven

THE GOLD BOX

"**R**eady to go get some supper now, Willy?" The last man had just left the room where Father Seelos was hearing Confessions. He came up and put his arm around Willy's shoulder and the two bundled up again to face the cold December air.

"I am hungry." Willy had been sitting in the church pew for what seemed like hours. He was tired and hungry. Father Seelos, though, looked refreshed and happy.

"Well, let us join the soldiers in their supper and then rest. Have you decided what you are going to do tomorrow?"

"I need to find a boat going back to Aquia Creek Landing. I'm sure the *Lady Jane* has already left."

"Well, we leave for Baltimore tomorrow evening. If you are heading that way, you are welcome to come with us."

"Oh, no, Father. But thank you. I need to get back to Fredericksburg and I couldn't ask any more of you. Here is your holy card back. I've learned the prayer."

Father Seelos shook his head. "Keep the holy card, Willy. It will remind you of God."

"It will remind me of you, too, Father." Father Seelos smiled.

They had reached the hospital and went inside for supper and rest.

The next morning, Willy went down to the dock to find a boat to take him back to Aquia Creek Landing. To his surprise, the *Lady Jane* was still in the harbor. He looked around for the familiar short and stocky frame of Frank. The uniforms worn by the sailors made them look so much alike; Willy had a hard time figuring out which of the sailors was Frank. This time, the men were loading supplies into the boat. Their work caused their breath to make little clouds in the cold air.

As Willy got closer to the boat, he recognized Frank in the work line loading up crates. Willy wedged in between Frank and the next sailor in line and began passing the crates.

Frank glanced up from his work, "Willy! I didn't expect to see you again! Did you find your brother-in-law?"

"No," Willy said. "The William Smith from Company B, 24th Michigan in the hospital is not the same William Smith from Company B, 24th Michigan who is my brother-in-law."

"Are you kidding?" Frank hesitated in his work to stare at Willy in disbelief. "You mean your brother-in-law is..."

"Yes, still at the front. He's probably in battle right now while I run a wild goose chase looking for the wrong William Smith."

"Well, if it makes you feel any better, the battle hasn't happened yet," Frank said. "But my guess is that it will be in the next day or so."

"How do you know?"

"Word has it that the pontoon boats are finally laid for the crossing of the Rappahannock in spite of constant rifle fire from the Rebs in the town. Burnside, who planned this whole thing, has lost the surprise attack, but plans to throw all his men right at the town. These supplies we're loading up now are back-ups for the battle. Oh, how I wish I could be in the battle. Guess I should have been a soldier rather than a sailor."

"Anyway, could I hitch a ride with you back to Aquia Creek Landing? Are you leaving right away? I want to get there as soon as possible."

"Not sure when we're shovin' off. It will probably be tomorrow."

"Any other boats leaving today?"

"That steamer over there is leaving tonight. But she's on her way to Baltimore." *That must be the boat Father Seelos was talking about*, Willy thought.

"Any others going to Aquia Creek Landing?"

"Nope.

"Maybe I should walk," Willy said, under his breath.

"Walk!" Frank said. "Are you crazy? Do you know how far it is? And through all Reb territory, too? You'd get there sooner taking the *Lady Jane* tomorrow. Besides, you make a fair good deck hand," Frank smiled as he handed another crate to Willy.

Willy worked in silence for a while, thinking. Nothing was turning out the way he had expected or hoped. He was hundreds of miles from home, chasing the wrong William Smith by foot and by boat while his brother-in-law was facing the battlefield and maybe even death because of his blunder. Willy longed for the peace of saying the Rosary in the church yesterday. There, his problems didn't seem so big. There, he just emptied his mind and concentrated on the prayers. Just then, he had an uncontrollable urge to return to the quiet pew and the dark, silent interior of the church.

"I have to go now," Willy said to Frank as he stepped out of the work line. "I'll be back tonight. Can you slip me into your bunk again?"

"Sure, no problem. As long as you bring Whiskers."

"I don't go anywhere without him," Willy called over his shoulders as he started for the chapel. "I'll be back at dusk."

It took a moment for Willy's eyes to adjust to the dimly lit interior of the church. At first, all he could see was the glow of the red candle hanging from the ceiling in the center of the front of the church. He thought the church was empty, but when his eyes adjusted, he saw another lone figure kneeling in the front pew, hands folded and eyes fixed on a gold box below the red glow of the candle. Willy knew at once that it was Father Seelos.

Willy didn't want to disturb the priest during his prayers, so he knelt down behind him and pulled out his Rosary. With each prayer and bead that slipped through his mind and hands, he felt the same peace he had felt yesterday. He knew, somehow, that everything would work out for the best. He also knew that he wasn't in charge of everything...something, or Someone else, was. He supposed this Someone else that he felt here in this church, was God. Saying these prayers had awakened in him a realization of something he had never felt before. He realized that there was a greater hand than any general's moving the world. This brought him peace. He looked up again at the

Willy meets Jesus in the Tabernacle

front of the church. Somehow, looking at the gold box below the red glowing candle was soothing. It called out to him in a way Willy couldn't describe. It was a feeling of happiness and well-being that he had never experienced before.

As he finished his Rosary, Father Seelos rose and began to walk out of the church. He saw Willy kneeling in the pew and smiled.

"Willy," he said in a half-whisper. "I looked for you this morning, but you had already left. I'm so pleased to find you here."

"Father, can I talk to you?"

"Certainly, Willy." Father always acted as if the person he was talking to was the most important person in the world. And despite his many obligations, he always gave his full attention to the person who needed him at that moment.

"What is that gold box?" Willy said pointing to the front of the church.

"That is the Tabernacle, Willy. We believe that Jesus, His Body, Blood, Soul and Divinity, live in the form of consecrated bread there. He is truly present in the Tabernacle as long as the sanctuary light," Father pointed to the red candle hanging from the ceiling, "is lit."

Willy listened, but wasn't sure whether he fully understood. All he really understood was the peace he got from the Tabernacle. "All I know, Father, is that I feel more peace here, praying in this church, than anywhere else."

Father Seelos smiled an understanding smile. "I know."

"When I came in here to pray my Rosary, I was very upset that I couldn't get back to Aquia Creek Landing as soon as possible. I've heard that there is going to be a big battle any day and I want to get back to my brother-in-law before the battle happens. I guess I came here to find a quiet place to figure out a way to get there today. But instead, while I was praying and looking at the gold box, I mean Tabernacle, I suddenly felt, deep inside, that it would be okay if I didn't get back to Aquia Creek Landing today."

"When you prayed, you were talking to God. But you were also doing something much more important, Willy."

"What's that, Father?"

"You were also listening to God." Father Seelos smiled.

"I guess so. Anyway, I felt much better after I realized it would be okay. I still want to get to Aquia Creek Landing as soon as possible, but I just know things will work out all right in the end."

"You're right, Willy, they will. I think you've grown up a lot on your journey and you've learned something that many grown men never learn."

"What's that, Father?"

"That God is in charge, not us. Our true victory is not in battle, but in our own wills. If we conquer our own selves, give ourselves over to God's charge, then we have true victory."

Willy thought about this for a moment. Again, he didn't fully understand, but he knew a little of what Father was talking about through the peace of letting go of his worries.

"I will be leaving this evening, Willy. But know that if ever you need a friend, I will be praying for you. If you are ever near Annapolis, Maryland, look me up at St. Mary's Seminary and I will be happy to see you. Who knows? I frequently go out and do parish missions through the states. Perhaps we will meet again?"

Willy loved how Father Seelos treated him as an equal. He talked to him as if he were a man rather than a boy. "I'd like that, Father."

Chapter Eight

THE JOURNEY CONTINUES

"What do you mean, we won't be leaving tomorrow?" Willy asked Frank when he arrived at the dock later that evening.

"Sorry, mate. That's our latest orders. I don't know why. I think there might be some trouble up at Aquia Landing. They want us to wait a day or two."

"Trouble? But that's why I need to get there as quickly as possible!"

"I know what you mean." Frank kicked a stone into the water. "I want to get there as badly as you do, but there isn't anything to be done about it. You're welcome to bunk with me again tonight. It was a lot warmer with you and Whiskers in my bunk."

Willy's mind was all jumbled. It seemed that every road he took to get to his brother-in-law was a dead end. He wanted so desperately to reach him and there seemed no way to do it. He had come so close so many times, only to be frustrated again and again.

"C'mon," Frank said, "a good night's sleep will make things seem better. There's nothing we can do about it. We don't run the war. Heck, when you're in the navy, you don't even run yourself."

Frank and Willy snuck up the plank to the deck of the *Lady Jane*, staying in the shadows and then slipping below deck. Frank's bunk-mates greeted Willy again. Frank, Willy, and Whiskers climbed into the bunk and huddled together for warmth. Frank nuzzled his face into Whiskers' fur and Whiskers licked his cheek. Frank's eyes closed as a happy smile came across his face.

Willy lay awake a long time, listening to the lapping of the waves against the outside of the boat. He was still upset that they wouldn't be leaving the next day. There had to be something he could do about it. Should he find another boat? He hadn't heard of any others going to Aquia Creek Landing the next day. Should he start out on foot? He had been told again and again that it was foolish to do so. He tossed and turned in the bunk, too confused to sleep. It was cold, too. Even with the two boys and a raccoon sharing a bunk, it was cold. Willy slipped his hands into his pockets. His fingers rested on Jim's Rosary beads. He started praying the prayers Father Seelos had taught him. The priest's words began to come back to him. He thought of the peace in the chapel in front of the Tabernacle. He thought of what Father had said about conquering himself and the greatest battle he would have to face was within him, not on a battlefield.

Willy wondered if this worry he was going through was caused by his own fears. He was afraid that he had come all this way for nothing. He was afraid that his brother-in-law would be dead or wounded if he didn't get to him in time. He was afraid that he would have failed his sister and uncle if he didn't send his brother-in-law home. Most of all, he was afraid that he wouldn't be able to do what a man needed to do and prove himself no longer a boy. He prayed the prayers of the Rosary as he thought about these things. He asked God and his guardian angel to help him do the things he wanted to do. Exhausted, he fell into a deep sleep.

When Willy awoke the next morning, the bunks were empty except for Whiskers, who was sitting next to Willy eating a bit of hardtack, the common bread of the soldier. Next to Whiskers were more hardtack and a bit of dried beef. Willy ate it.

Frank appeared at the entryway to the cabin. "Everyone's at breakfast now, if you want to go back to the fort, or you can stay here. Word is that we are supposed to shove off tomorrow."

The only person Willy wanted to see at the fort was Father Seelos, but he had sailed on the steamer for Baltimore the night before. Still, there was one other place he wanted to visit, the chapel.

"Sure, I'll spend the day at the fort and meet you here at dusk," Willy said.

That evening again found Willy, Frank and Whiskers huddled together in the bunk. It was another cold night. The ice, even on the Chesapeake Bay, was so bad it delayed their sailing in the morning. "The Potomac is liable to be partially frozen, too," Frank said. "We'll have a hard time getting the *Lady Jane* up to Aquia."

Yet another delay! Willy sighed and instinctively reached for his Rosary. After spending most of the day in the chapel yesterday, he worried less about reaching his brother-in-law in time. He had come to realize that he was doing all he could and the rest was out of his hands.

The boat began to move slowly through the Bay up the river. Frank came down to the cabin during a break, totally exhausted. "It's taking all of us to keep the boat away from the worst of the ice. It's going to take us all day to reach Aquia."

"I know all about boats and ice," Willy said. "Lake Erie freezes a lot. Maybe I can help?"

"Don't risk it. Captain just might throw you off."

"Or maybe he'd be grateful for the extra hand."

Frank shrugged. "Suit yourself."

Willy joined Frank on the deck. It was nearly an hour before the Captain realized that one of his sailors wasn't wearing a uniform.

"You there! What are you doing on my boat?"

"Just thanking you for the ride, Captain."

"Who do you think you are? No civilians are allowed on my boat!"

"Aw, Cap, let him stay," one of the sailors yelled. "He's been on boats before. He knows what he's doing."

"Yeah, Cap. We need all the hands we can get."

The Captain glared at Willy. "You ever been on a boat before, son?"

"I've helped my brother-in-law run a ferry on Lake Erie."

"Lake Erie! Boy, are you a long way from home. Okay, boy, you can stay." Willy and Frank grinned at each other. "But only until Aquia Creek Landing. Then you're on your own." The Captain started to walk away, then turned to glance at Willy again. "That is," he said, "unless you want to enlist in the U.S. Navy. Perhaps we could use another powder monkey."

"Thank you, sir. I have other business I have to attend to."

The Captain shrugged. "Suit yourself."

The *Lady Jane* pulled into Aquia Creek Landing after dusk. Again, the night was bitterly cold and Willy didn't need much convincing to spend it with Frank and Whiskers. He was so exhausted after the day's work on the boat, he knew he had to get some rest before the long walk to Fredericksburg the next day.

Frank held Whiskers and stood looking at Willy the next morning, unwilling to say their goodbyes. Finally, Frank handed Whiskers to Willy. "Thanks, Frank, for all you've done for me." Frank stood stroking Whiskers' fur.

"Naw. I didn't do anything."

"Well, I guess I better get going." Willy stuck out his hand. The two boys shook and Willy turned quickly to go. Several of the other sailors called their goodbyes to Willy and he turned and waved one last time as the bustling landing grew smaller.

Willy had a long walk ahead of him, but the road was far from lonely. Soldiers on horseback, on foot, in wagons and carts hurried past him going in both directions. Willy heard bits and pieces of conversations along the road. It seemed that the Union Army had occupied the town a couple of days before, driving the Rebels to the high ground beyond. General Burnside was hoping to attack the Rebs on three fronts to take the high ground, but no one seemed to know whether he had done it or not. Although Willy's feet carried him toward the battlefield as quickly as they could, he didn't feel the same worry and dread about getting there too late. He had done what he could and knew the rest was out of his hands. Was this the strange peace that Father Seelos had talked to him about? Was this the victory over his own fear and wants that the priest had said would come with prayer? For what seemed like the hundredth time since Father Seelos had left Fortress Monroe, Willy wished his could see and talk to him again.

Several times Willy and Whiskers had to jump off the main road when a horse or wagon sped by. Besides that, the weather had warmed a bit and the road was beginning to get muddy. Willy was wondering if he'd ever reach the battle.

Late in the afternoon, he began to hear it — low rumbling at first, like a thunderstorm in the distance. As they got closer to the Rappahannock, the rumbling got louder. The road got more crowded, so that Willy was rarely on the road itself, but walking alongside it in the woods. A clearing opened in front of Willy and he could see a house with some tents surrounding it. As he approached the house, horses continually rode up to it, delivered something to the soldier at the door, and then rode away. Willy wondered if this could be General Burnside's headquarters. He approached one of the soldiers standing outside the house.

"Excuse me, is this the headquarters of the Army of the Potomac?" Willy asked.

"Yes," the man said, distracted by another message from another soldier on a horse. Having received the message, the man suddenly looked down at Willy.

"Boy, you better get out of here. Don't you know there's a battle going on? Can't you hear the cannon fire? What are you doing here, anyway? I thought all the civilians left days ago."

"I'm here to find my brother-in-law. He's in the 24th Michigan. Are they in the fight?"

"'Course they're in the fight!" the soldier said impatiently. "The whole army's in the fight. We're throwing over 100,000 men at the Rebs today, boy."

"Where's the 24th Michigan? Do you know?"

"They're one of that all-Western brigade, aren't they?"

"I think so." Willy thought they were, but didn't know for sure.

"They're first corps, the far left grand division." The man pointed toward the south. "They all crossed the river two days ago."

"Thanks!" Willy began to trot down the road.

"Say, you can't go that way!" the soldier called after him. "They're across the river! That's restricted for civilians! Fool kid!"

Willy ignored the soldier and continued to trot toward the river. Dusk was falling when he finally reached the riverbank. Two rows of pontoon bridges spanned the river toward the opposite shore. Soldiers stood at either end of the river, guarding the bridges. How was he supposed to get past the guards to the other side? The cannon fire had all but stopped with the coming of the darkness. Willy thought that the noise would have been better than the eerie silence of the cold, dark night. He was standing behind a tree deciding what to do when a wagon went down the steep embankment going toward the pontoon bridges. He ran in the shadow of the tree and hopped into the back of the wagon, lying low so he wouldn't be seen.

The wagon was stopped at the bridge. "Come to pick up the wounded from the left flank," the driver said to the soldiers guarding the pontoon. Willy felt the wagon bump onto the bridge and rattle across the boards. It slowed again before bumping back up to the shore on the opposite side. It went upwards sharply before it met more level road beyond the river. Willy thought he better get off the wagon soon before he was mistaken for a wounded soldier and shipped off to the hospital. The wagon began to slow and Willy hopped off. He kept to the shadows, so he wouldn't be seen.

The wagon had pulled up to a large white tent. Around the tent were all sorts of wounded men. Some were missing arms or legs, some had heads bandaged, some wore bloody bandages around their stomachs or chests. Soldiers lifted the men up and set them in the wagon one by one. With each movement, the men let out the most agonizing cries. Willy searched each face, expecting to see his brother-in-law among the wounded. It was difficult to

Willy hitches a ride across the pontoon bridge

make out the men's features in the dim light. He didn't recognize any of the wounded.

Willy left the army hospital and went to find his brother-in-law's regiment. He had no idea where he was going and was afraid to ask anyone directions to the 24th Michigan. The night was bitterly cold. It was like time itself was frozen in a never-ending battlefield of stillness. He kept to the shadows as best he could. He came across a group of men crouched in trenches. No campfire or shelter protected them from the cold night. He crouched next to a man in the ditch. The man moved slightly as if awakened from a nap.

"Excuse me," Willy whispered to the man, knowing somehow that he needed to be quiet. "Is this the 24th Michigan?"

The man looked at him without really seeing him. The moon had come out and lit the man's face. To Willy, the man's face looked blank, like he was afraid to think. "Yep, this is the 24th."

Willy's heart was pounding. Finally, a stroke of good luck! He had found the 24th Michigan. "I'm looking for William Smith of Company B"

"Company B? They're here somewhere, I suppose. Try up the trench a bit." The man hesitated, "Say, aren't you a little young to be a soldier?"

"I don't think so," Willy responded as he made his way up the trench. "Company B?" he asked another soldier, who pointed further up the trench. "Company B?" he asked another.

"Company B, here. Who wants to know?"

"I'm looking for William Smith," Willy said, ignoring the question.

"I'm William Smith. Who wants to know?"

Could it be, after all this time, that he finally found his brother-in-law? And he was still alive!

Chapter Nine

THE GOOD REB

"Bill? Is it you?" Willy asked, crouching down in the trench.

"Who is it?" Willy's brother-in-law said. "Who's looking for me?" The moon began to shine brighter on the men in blue crouching in the trenches. Willy saw the face of his brother-in-law in the moonlight. It was smeared with dirt and had the stubble of a beard on his chin and cheeks, but otherwise, he looked unhurt. Willy's heart leapt in thanksgiving.

"Bill, it's me, Willy," Willy said, holding his breath.

"Willy! Willy McBlaine? How'd you get here, boy?"

"Walked. Hitched the train. Even came by boat part of the way."

The other soldiers began to crowd around the boy, all talking at once. Willy recognized many of the Trenton Boys from back home — John Pardington, Eli McInerny and so many others that had signed up with his brother-in-law. Willy was so glad to see them alive.

"Quiet down back there," a commanding voice ordered the men. "What is this, a family reunion?"

"Sorry, Sarge," Bill said. The men started whispering.

"How's Sarah? And baby Mariah?" John Pardington asked.

"How are my folks? When did you last see them? Can you go back and tell them we're okay?" The questions came in quick, urgent whispers. The only one who didn't talk was Willy's brother-in-law, Bill.

When Willy had answered everyone's questions, Bill finally spoke. "I got a letter from your sister that you up and left. She's worried sick about you, you know. Why'd you come?"

"I came to get you," Willy said.

"I can't leave here. We're in the middle of a war. Heck, we're in the middle of a battle here."

"But Liz needs you. Ever since the baby's been born, she's been sick something terrible."

"She's not said anything about a sickness in her letters," Bill said.

"She probably didn't want to worry you. That's why I had to come."

"How is she ailing? What's wrong with her?"

"She just sits around all day with the baby. Sometimes she cries. Sometimes she takes to her bed."

"Sounds like she's just got a bad case of the blues. Happens when you have a baby, sometimes," John added. "Sarah had a touch of it, too, after Mariah was born. They get over it okay, usually.

"I don't think having you leave helped her at all," Bill scolded Willy. "Why'd you think coming here would help?"

Willy held his breath for a second and blurted out, "I want to take your place here at the front, Bill. I want to be a soldier and let you go home to my sister and your son."

The men within hearing distance muffled chuckles in their hands. Willy looked at them, surprised that they thought he was kidding.

"I'm serious. I am going to be a soldier and take your place, Bill."

Bill was slowly shaking his head. "I don't know how you managed to come all this way by yourself, Willy. And there's no doubt that you would hold your own in a fight, but you're not taking my place."

"Why not?"

"We saw our first battle today, Willy," Bill began to explain. "We saw men's heads blown clean off from their bodies. We saw our own men fall in a shower of bullets and cannon fire. War is not the glory you are looking for. It is blood and courage and fear and sleeping long cold nights in trenches."

"But you said I could hold my own in a battle," Willy protested.

"That you could. And that is the reason I left you in charge of your sister when I came to this war. You have to be her strength. My country needs me to save the Union, but I need you to save my family." Bill paused for a second. "And you've let me down, Willy."

Of all the scenes that Willy had thought about after finally finding his brother-in-law, this one had never occurred to him. He never thought that his sister needed him more than she needed her husband. He felt like he had let everyone down. His whole journey had been a total failure from the very first step.

Bill seemed to understand his silence. "I don't mean to be harsh on you, boy. I know you did what you did out of love and concern for your sister. But out of love for her, you have to go back now." Willy started to argue and then stopped. He knew that what Bill had said was the truth. As hard as it was for Willy to hear, he knew he couldn't argue with his brother-in-law. Willy nodded slowly. The time for arguing about it had passed. Willy's hand reached into his pocket where he found his Rosary. He squeezed it hard so that the tears brimming in his eyes didn't run down his cheeks.

"Stay here tonight. At least huddled together we can try to stay warm. Tomorrow, I'll send you to the nearest train back to Michigan. Don't forget to give my wife and child a kiss for me. And tell them that I love them."

The next morning, Bill got permission to walk Willy back across the pontoon bridge to the army headquarters on the far side of the river. As they reached the high ground at Stafford Heights, they met a group of men looking through a spyglass at the opposite shore. The men wore the red baggy pants and felt hats that Willy had seen before. In fact, one of them was his old pal, Jim Jenkins.

"Jim!" Willy called as he ran up to him.

"Why, I'll be," Jim said, scratching his head. "It's my little pal with the powerful guardian angel. Is this your brother-in-law, Willy?"

"Yes. I finally found him. He was here all the time. The fellow in the hospital at Fortress Monroe was another William Smith." Bill and Jim shook hands.

"Nice to meet a relative to this little determined soldier," Jim said. Willy hung his head. "Aren't you joining up, now?" Jim asked him.

"No," Bill said. "He's on his way to a train to take him back to Michigan."

"Oohh," Jim nodded slowly. He put a spyglass to his eye and looked across the river.

Willy and Bill looked over their shoulders, but all they could see was the ruins of the town and the high ground beyond.

Angel of Marye's Heights helps wounded soldiers

"There he is. Yep, he's giving another one a drink. This time it's one of ours," another soldier with an eyeglass was saying. "Do you see him, Jim?"

"I see him," Jim replied.

"And no one's firing on him?" another said.

"No. He just keeps going from one to another giving water and putting a knapsack under his head."

"What's going on?" Bill asked.

"There's a Reb soldier over on Marye's Heights taking care of the wounded there."

"What's so special about that?" Bill asked.

"He has two army's guns trained on his every move. There's been no truce called and we're waiting the order to charge the Rebs a fourth time."

"Most of the wounded are Union Army from the first three charges yesterday," Jim said.

"You mean the wounded have been there all night?" Willy asked, wide-eyed.

"Most of yesterday and all the night." Jim handed his spy-glass to Willy. "Want to see an angel in action, boy?" Willy looked through the glass and trained it on the hill on the opposite shore. It took a second to focus. "No, close the other eye, you'll be able to see better."

What Willy saw was a field of blue, white and red. The soldiers' blue uniforms were splattered in red completely covering the field. Some of the wounds were too awful to look at. Most of the soldiers were not moving at all, but some moved slightly. All had a white layer of frost on them from the previous bitter cold night. Finally, Willy saw a man in a butternut-colored uniform moving among the sea of blue. He gave one wounded soldier a drink and put his knapsack under his head like a pillow. As Willy scanned the field below where the wounded and dead lay, he saw the Union Army. Many had guns pointed at the Reb helping the men, but none were firing. Most just looked at him with solemn expressions. Willy moved the glass up the hill to where the Confederate Army was positioned. If it hadn't been for the color of the uniforms, one could not have told the difference between the two armies. The men looked the same. Even the expressions on their faces as they watched the Angel of Marye's Heights move among the wounded, were the same.

It reminded Willy of what Father Seelos had said about seeing the soldiers as men, also loved by God, and not the enemy to be hated. Certainly, this Reb soldier didn't hate the Yanks he was helping on the battlefield. Willy handed the spy-glass to his brother-in-law.

"That man is an angel," Jim said.

"And has a great guardian angel, too," Willy added.

Jim smiled. "Safe journey, Willy. God be with you."

Willy and Bill said their goodbyes at the army head-quarters. Word was that the battle of Fredericksburg was a complete failure. The Union Army was to withdraw quietly over the pontoon bridges that night. They were already lay-ing pine needles on the bridge so they wouldn't make so much noise. Willy thought it was just like his whole journey. It was a complete failure. He was quietly going back home after his long fight to get there. The army's mood matched his own. His brother-in-law gave him some money for the train and some more to give to his sister before they said their good-byes. He rode in a wagon train full of wounded back north to Washington City and then caught a train that would take him home. Like the army, he felt shame in his failure. He reached into his pocket and squeezed his Rosary. Still, he didn't feel like praying. Why did God let him go all the way there, only to fail his mission?

Chapter Ten

MISSION ACCOMPLISHED

"Willy!" Willy was lost in thought and in the motion of the train and didn't respond the first time his name was called. "Willy! Is that you?" The second time he heard his name, Whiskers popped out of his knapsack and licked his face to get his attention. Willy looked around the train to see who was calling his name. Two men dressed all in black with four-cornered pointed hats stood before him.

"Father Seelos!" Willy exclaimed. It was the first time since finding his brother-in-law that Willy was really excited.

The two priests sat on the bench next to Willy. "What are you doing here, Willy? Did you ever find your brother-in-law? Is he all right?"

Willy looked down at his hands. "Yes, I did find him," he began slowly. "I found him in the trenches at Fredericksburg. He was fine, but he wouldn't come home. He said my job was at home taking care of my sister and nephew and his job was to fight in the army."

Father Seelos nodded slowly. "I see. And you didn't like that answer?"

"No. It felt like my whole trip has been wasted. I failed in my mission."

"Perhaps you didn't fail in your mission," Father Seelos said. "Perhaps you just thought your mission was something different than it was."

"What do you mean, Father?"

"You'll find out in time, Willy. Your quest is not yet over, I think."

Willy looked puzzled.

"Forgive me, I forgot to introduce to you my companion, Father Giesen. Father, this is Willy McBlaine, traveling from Virginia back to his home in Michigan."

"Pleased to meet you, son," Father Giesen said in a thick German accent.

"Where are you going, Father?" Willy asked.

"We are on our way to Ohio to give a parish mission."

"Where in Ohio?"

"Toledo. We hear it is a rough town."

"I'm getting off in Toledo, too, and taking the ferry to Trenton," Willy said.

"Why don't you come to our talk the first day of the mission?" Father Seelos suggested.

"I don't know, Father. My brother-in-law wanted me home pretty quickly."

"But you are not anxious to get home, are you, Willy?"

"No." Willy hung his head.

"Maybe one day of a mission will help you get ready. What do you think? It couldn't hurt, could it?"

Father Seelos' cheerfulness was spreading. Willy couldn't help but feel better since the pleasant priest sat next to him. Certainly listening to Father Seelos would be better than facing his sister and uncle when he returned home, not to mention the ridicule of his friends to whom he had boasted that he was going to join the army.

"You're right, Father. A day at your mission couldn't hurt. I just hope your mission is more successful than mine was."

"We always pray for a good mission," Father Seelos said. "Do you remember how to say the Rosary?"

"Yes," Willy said slowly.

"But you haven't been praying it, have you?"

"No." Father Seelos seemed to read Willy's mind.

"Well, why don't we say one together?" The two priests pulled out their long strings of black beads and Willy brought out his shiny ones from his pocket. As they said the Rosary, the worries seemed to flow out of Willy's mind with the prayers. He felt better with every slip of a bead through his fingers.

The only kind of mission Willy knew about was the kind he had just failed. He had no idea what kind of mission the priests were on. Maybe their mission was to get the people to pray more? Even after Father Seelos had explained a little bit about the mission, Willy wasn't sure what the point of it was exactly. Willy remembered the rough lake town of Toledo. It wouldn't be very easy to get some of the people to pray.

After many hours and delays, the train finally pulled into Toledo. Father Seelos invited Willy to stay with the priests in whatever place the parish had prepared for them. Willy gratefully accepted.

Early the next morning, both priests were up and dressed for Mass. Willy was rubbing his eyes, trying to focus on the black figures rushing around the room.

"We will be saying the early Mass, Willy. Would you like to join us?" Father Seelos asked.

"Uh, sure," Willy replied.

The sun was barely lifting over the gray horizon when the priests and Willy walked into the church across the alley from the small building in which they were staying. A few elderly ladies and shabbily dressed men, bundled in scarves and cloaks, filtered into the darkened church. Willy slipped into the back pew as the priests went to get ready for Mass.

There, in the cold, dark interior of the church, a glow that seemed to radiate from the red candle in front of the gold box...what did Father call it? The Tabernacle...the glow from the light seemed to push away the cold, first from Willy's heart, then from his head. The warmth began to creep over his whole body. Father Seelos came out and began the Mass. Willy didn't understand anything that was said, but he seemed to sense what was being done. He understood, somehow, that what was happening on the altar was the most important thing he had ever seen in his life. Father Giesen assisted Father Seelos and together they accomplished what Willy thought must have been a miracle.

He looked around at the worn and tired faces around him. The people themselves even looked transformed, glowing in the warmth of the red candle and the special motions on the altar.

Before Willy knew it, the Mass had ended and the priests were taking Willy to breakfast. Over their meal, Willy asked why the Mass seemed so special. Father Seelos already knew that Willy had known nearly nothing about religion. He started from the beginning.

"God created man in the persons of Adam and Eve and wanted them to live with Him forever in Paradise. But they disobeyed God and were thrown out of Paradise. God still loved mankind and wanted him to come into heaven and live with Him forever, so He sent His only Son, Jesus, to die for our sins and open the gates of heaven. The Son's love was more pleasing to God than our sins are displeasing to Him. At the Mass, we re-present that loving sacrifice of Jesus in payment for our sins. That is why it feels so special."

Willy nodded and thought about it. He furrowed his brow. "Then the Mass is important because it keeps the sacrifice of Jesus ever here and now?"

"Yes. Excellent, Willy. There are many Catholics who don't understand that. Our sins crucified Jesus and still do."

"What is the white thing you give to people near the end?" Willy asked.

"It is Holy Communion. It is the Body, Blood, Soul and Divinity of Jesus."

"Oh, it is what is in the Tabernacle," Willy said carefully.

"Excellent again, Willy. Yes."

"Can I receive Holy Communion sometime?" Willy asked.

The two priests looked at each other. "Well, Willy, the 'communion' part of Holy Communion means that we all believe in the same thing. We have been prepared to understand to the best of our abilities, the mysteries and teachings of the Church. Sometimes it takes years of preparation before a person is allowed to receive that special grace."

"Oh," Willy was disappointed. Years of study? He knew that wouldn't happen if he were back in Trenton. He wondered where the nearest Catholic church was in

85

Trenton, anyway. He had never noticed one before. "So what is next for this 'mission?'" Willy asked.

"This afternoon we hear Confessions. Tonight we preach and hear more Confessions," Father Seelos said.

"How do you know when your mission is accomplished?" Willy asked.

Both priests laughed. "Sometimes we don't know. Our goal is to get the people to be serious about their faith. To love God and know He loves them. To go to church often and say their prayers at home and live a good Catholic life everywhere. That is our mission."

"It sounds harder than going from Michigan to Virginia to fight in the army," Willy smiled.

Again the priests laughed. "Sometimes it is, Willy."

Willy hung around the church most of the day watching the people trickle in to have their Confessions heard and their sins absolved by the priests. Some of the people came out of the confessional boxes crying, others smiling. Very few came out with the same sour looks they seemed to carry when they went in. Willy had a longing to go into the box and receive absolution for his sins, too. He thought it would feel good to hear the words of forgiveness. He thought it would certainly feel better than facing his uncle and sister in the next day or two.

That evening, the church was about half full for the priest's preaching. Father Seelos talked about the mercy and love of God. He wore a large crucifix around his neck that he held it the entire time he talked, drawing the people's attention to it from time to time. His words warmed Willy's heart. He never knew he was so loved. It made him want to do something for God, who loved him so much.

Father Seelos celebrates Mass during a parish mission

After the talk, the Fathers again heard Confessions. The lines were longer this time.

"Well, I guess you'll be leaving us tomorrow, Willy," Father said when they returned to their room that evening.

"I was thinking, Father, that maybe I could stay another day?"

"You aren't avoiding what is waiting for you at home, are you, Willy?" Father Seelos seemed to see right through him.

"Well, maybe. But I really would like to spend another day here at the parish mission."

"I suppose that would be all right," Father Seelos said.

Willy ended up staying more than a day; he stayed the whole week. Every day, more and more people came to the mission. The morning Masses were now packed and the lines to the confessional seemed never to end. Most of all, Willy now had a hunger in his heart for Holy Communion and to receive the other Sacraments Father Seelos talked about. But how could he, a boy who had never even been baptized, who had never been taught about religion, become a Catholic in such a short period of time? He waited for the right time to approach Father Seelos, who had become busier and busier as the week wore on.

The last afternoon of the mission, Father Seelos took a break from hearing Confessions. He said he had heard 300 Confessions that week. Willy didn't doubt that at all.

"Father, can I ask you something?" Willy began.

"Anything, Willy."

"Can you baptize me?"

A large smile came across Father Seelos' pleasant face. "If you desire Baptism, Willy, I will baptize you. But Baptism means that you have promised to live your faith. Do you think you can do that in a family that is not of your faith?"

"I've thought about it long and hard, Father. I will find a priest in Trenton to continue my instruction. I'm ready to face my uncle and my sister and apologize to them for causing them worry and grief. I know now that I was thinking mostly of myself and the glory I would find in war and what a hero I would be if I took my brother-in-law's place. It was selfish of me."

"Don't be too hard on yourself, Willy. You are brave. You are determined. And this is the reason I will baptize you because I know that when you set your mind to something, you will not falter. Despite all the obstacles put in your way, you will become the best Catholic you can be."

Willy beamed. Father Seelos' praise was just what he needed. They began to walk arm and arm toward the church for the Baptism.

"So, Father, how do you think the mission went this week?" Willy asked.

Father looked directly into Willy's eyes and grinned. "Mission accomplished."

Chapter Eleven

VICTORY!

Lake Erie was frozen. Willy would have to return home on foot or by train. He counted his money. Just enough for the train fare and not much left over. For some reason, ever since his Baptism, he had been really anxious to return home. The priests' mission was over for the parish in Toledo and they were leaving the next day for another Ohio town. Willy knew it was time to go home.

"I've asked around, Willy. There is a Catholic church in Trenton," Father Seelos said. "It is St. Joseph's on 3rd Street. The pastor is a Father Henry. Give him this letter from me. He will continue to instruct you so that you will soon be ready for your First Confession and First Communion."

Willy shook the priest's hand as he took the letter. "Yes, I know where it is. I passed it often enough, but just didn't think much about it," Willy said. "Thank you for everything, Father. I think I know now why I came on this journey. Sometimes I feel like it is just beginning rather than nearing an end."

"Very true, Willy. The Christian journey never ends until we reach heaven."

"Will I ever see you again, Father?"

"Our Redemptorist priests do parish missions all over this territory. I'm sure that we will be traveling to Michigan before too long. I think we will see each other again, Willy."

Willy smiled as he hopped on the train bound toward Michigan and home.

Whiskers walked alongside Willy as they approached his uncle's house. It was the middle of the afternoon, so Willy knew his uncle would be at the mill until suppertime. His sister would be at home, though.

Before he could reach the front porch of the small clapboard framed house, the door flew open and Elizabeth ran out.

"Willy! You're home! You're home!" Elizabeth's arms wrapped the boy in warmth. Willy choked back tears. He never expected such a warm welcome.

His sister was crying. "Oh, I thought I'd lost you forever, Willy! Thank God you are safe. Oh, but you look so tired and hungry. Come in and get warmed and fed."

Willy followed his sister into the house. She, too, looked worn, but not as desperately sick as he remembered her when he had left two months ago. She seemed tired, but more alive than before. She was no longer wasting away. Willy wondered what had changed in his absence.

When Willy walked into the house, he saw his tiny nephew asleep in the cradle. He had grown so much in the last two months. Willy could hardly believe it. "Little Willy has gotten so big!" he said.

His sister looked at her son and smiled. Willy hadn't seen that smile since before Little Willy was born. She looked almost radiant again. "Yes, he has. And he looks just like his Pa, don't you think?"

"He does," Willy agreed.

"Oh, Willy, I got a letter from Bill who said you had been to see him to try to get him to come home to us. What a brave thing to do. Brave, but foolish. We were so worried!"

"I'm sorry I worried you," Willy said, taking off his knapsack, hat and cloak and settling himself in front of a bowl of steaming stew.

"But something happened to me when you left," Elizabeth said. "I thought I no longer wanted to live...Bill gone, you gone and the baby sick. I... I..." Elizabeth hesitated. "I began to pray."

"Pray? I didn't know you knew how to!"

"Our parents taught us before they died. You were too young to remember, but I remembered some of the prayers they taught me and how much I loved kneeling around our home altar at night with the candle glow warming my heart as I prayed."

"You are right, I don't remember." Willy was amazed. His sister had never talked about life before they came to live with their uncle.

"Uncle never wanted to pray, so I stopped," Elizabeth continued. "He doesn't like it that I pray now, but he sees how it has helped me. Oh, and there's something else. I've started to go to church, too."

"Really?" Willy said. "A church here in Trenton?"

"Yes. I visited them all and I know the one I belonged in was St. Joseph's. I've asked Father Henry there to give me instruction so I can become Catholic."

Willy's heart skipped a beat. His sister was going to take instruction from Father Henry!

"Oh, Elizabeth! I can't believe it!" Willy nearly shouted.

"I know. I know," Elizabeth sounded apologetic. "It isn't like our family to be religious, but it was my only answer."

"No, Elizabeth, you won't believe what happened to me on my trip!" Willy poured forth his whole story, from meeting Jim Jenkins, learning how to pray, learning all he had from Father Seelos, attending the mission and being baptized. Elizabeth's eyes got wider and wider as he talked.

After Willy finished his story, Elizabeth rushed to him and took his hands in her own. "Oh, don't you see, Willy? This was all meant to be. We will be able to go to church together and love each other just as Jesus loved us."

Willy smiled at his sister's enthusiasm. "But what will Uncle say about all this?" Willy asked, his smile fading.

"He's accepted it so far. Father Henry says the only way to act toward Uncle is to love him. He says that my, now our, example will soften his heart."

Willy wasn't sure, but he was willing to give it a try. Just then, Uncle John came through the door. He stopped and stared at Willy for a second.

"Well, you're back. Have a nice little adventure?" Uncle John was a large man, with large, rough hands that had seen hard work. He didn't like weak and soft things.

"I'm sorry I worried you, Uncle," Willy began.

"Worried your sister more, I'd say," Uncle said as he hung up his cloak and hat. "Stew smells good, Elizabeth. I'm starved."

Uncle John sat at the table as Elizabeth set a bowl in front of him. "Glad you're back, though," he said without looking at Willy. Willy smiled at Elizabeth. "Could use an extra hand around here."

"Yes, Uncle. Anything I can do to make up for being away, I'll do."

Uncle John looked at Willy to see if he was being truthful. Willy smiled.

"There's something different about you, boy. Something happen to you on your trip?"

"Lots of things happened, Uncle. I suppose you could say I grew up a lot on the trip."

"I'd say so," Uncle John responded.

The next few weeks, Willy, Elizabeth and the baby met with Father Henry several times. By the spring, they were ready to receive their Sacraments. Uncle John still thought the religious stuff was for fools, but he couldn't deny that things at home were much better since his niece and nephew had been attending St. Joseph's. The home was happy and friendly. Chores were done without even asking and the house and property was always clean and cheery. The change couldn't help but affect Uncle John.

At breakfast one sunny morning, Elizabeth tested her uncle's new pleasant frame of mind. "Sunday is the day for Willy and me to receive our First Communion, Uncle." Uncle John just nodded. "Will you come with us to church?"

"What!" Uncle John nearly jumped up from the table. "Me! Inside a church? Forget it!"

"Please, Uncle," Willy joined in. "It is very special to Elizabeth and me. Please come." Uncle John looked from one pleading face to another.

"All right. But just this once."

"Thank you, Uncle. Thank you!"

The big day came and Willy could hardly contain his excitement. He knew now that this was the reason for his journey to Virginia and back. He couldn't change the fate of the army through battle, but he could win souls for Christ, especially his own. Without the journey, without Father Seelos' kindness and careful instruction, Willy would not be receiving Jesus in his soul this day.

And there next to him in the pew was his sister and there was his Uncle John, looking uncomfortable in a suit and combed hair. What a victory it was to be there with them on this day!

When Willy knelt at the altar to receive Jesus on his tongue, he knew that his mission was a success. He had found the victory he had sought!

An American Saint

Blessed Francis Xavier Seelos

Francis Xavier Seelos was born on January 11, 1819 in Fussen which is part of Germany. He was baptized the same day at the parish church of St. Mang. His father was a stocking maker and his mother a homemaker. Francis, who was called Xavier by his family, grew up in a happy, loving home. From a young age, he felt the calling to the priesthood. He entered the seminary in his homeland of Germany and soon felt drawn to the order of priests called the Congregation of the Most Holy Redeemer, or Redemptorists. They conducted parish missions to renew the people in their faith. Their particular focus was on the German immigrants to the United States. Francis had a desire to go to the United States to be a part of the German parish renewal.

Francis arrived in New York on April 20, 1843, and on December 22, 1844, was ordained a priest in the Redemptorist Church of St. James in Baltimore, Maryland. Right after he was ordained, Father Seelos was sent to Pittsburgh were he worked for nine years in the parish of St. Philomena's with the pastor, St. John Neumann. He often said that Father Neumann showed him how to be truly holy. St. Philomena's must have been a holy place with two future saints living in the rectory at the same time!

Father Seelos was known for his kindness and cheerful disposition. He loved bringing the faithful to a fuller knowledge of Christ through the sacraments and teaching catechism. He was also in charge of the growing Redemptorist seminary and was eventually moved to the seminary in Cumberland, Maryland, right before the Civil War. Father Seelos moved the seminarians to Annapolis in

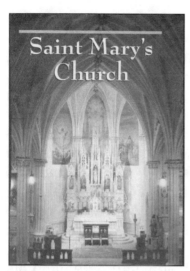

*St. Mary's, Annapolis
Home of the
Redemptorist Seminary
in 1860*

1862 after the Battle of Antietam, which took place near Cumberland. Father Seelos thought that Annapolis would be a safer place for his future priests. The seminarians were always in danger of being drafted into the army. Father Seelos even went to Washington, DC to ask President Abraham Lincoln to release his future priests from going to war. Although President Lincoln didn't make any promises to Father Seelos, Father Seelos was impressed by the friendly manner of the president. In the end, Father Seelos was successful in keeping his priests off the battlefield and in the churches.

During the war, Father Seelos did his part to serve those troops serving the United States. The trip Father Seelos made to the army hospital in this story was only one of many such trips he documented through letters to his family back in Germany. He also conducted missions throughout the Northeast and Midwestern United States.

After the Civil War, Father Seelos was stationed for a while in Michigan. Again, he traveled through the Midwest giving parish missions. He was transferred to New Orleans in 1868. Here he was well known for his kindness and charity to all. When a yellow fever epidemic broke out in New Orleans, Father Seelos gave himself tirelessly to serve those who had been stricken by the disease. He himself caught the sickness and died as he had lived, serving his flock.

On April 9, 2000, Pope John Paul II beatified Francis Xavier Seelos.

Willy McBlaine is a fictional character based on a true-life relative of the author. The author's great-great-great-great grandfather was William Smith, of Company B, 24th Michigan, of the Iron Brigade. Bill Smith was married to Elizabeth McBlaine. William Smith survived Fredericksburg and several other battles. He lost his arm on the first day of the Battle of Gettysburg, July 1st, 1863, and was discharged. He returned to Trenton, Michigan, where he and his wife, Elizabeth, raised their family. They moved to Detroit where William Smith became a customs agent. Many of his friends from Trenton, Michigan, were not so fortunate. John Pardington, who drew the picture on this page of the "Trenton Boys," which included William Smith, for a letter home to his wife, died at Gettysburg, leaving his young wife and daughter alone. Many thanks to Coralou Peel Lassen, the direct descendant of John Pardington, who was kind enough to share her family's history with the author's family.

There really were two William Smiths in Company B of the 24th Michigan. The other William Smith was from

This drawing is from a letter by John Pardington to his wife, Sarah. It shows "The Trenton Boys," including Bill Smith. John was killed at the Battle of Gettysburg.

101

Detroit and was discharged for pneumonia in December of 1862, without fighting in any battles.

The Iron Brigade fought hard at the Battle of Gettysburg. Their dead were among the first casualties of the battle.

Different sets of troops in the army had different types of uniforms. Most of the Union army wore blue, and most of the Confederate army wore butternut or gray. But among the individual regiments, there were distinct differences, like the Zouave uniform worn by Jim in the story or the tall black hats worn by the Iron Brigade.

Fortress Monroe still sits at the opening of Hampton Roads. Father Seelos actually did visit the sick men in the hospital there right before the Battle of Fredericksburg and offered them words of comfort and the sacraments.

Blessed Francis Seelos, Cheerful Lover of Souls, teach us to love one another as our Master has loved us!

The Whole Picture

A Civil War Unit Study

The story of the American Civil War can't be told in one book, or even in a hundred and one books. The war began officially when a U.S.-held fort off the coast of South Carolina was taken from the U.S. Army by South Carolina, which had just decided to separate from the United States. Some people say it was the right of the state to drop out of the United States; others say that South Carolina and the other Southern states that joined her, simply wanted to make sure they were allowed to own black people as slaves. The Northern states didn't have slaves and the issue had divided the country between North and South, also known as the Union and Confederacy.

The war raged from 1861 to 1865. President Abraham Lincoln led the Union during the entire time. The Confederate president was Jefferson Davis. Both the Union and Confederates thought the war would be a short one. The Union had more men and better equipment, since many of the country's manufacturing plants were located in the North. The Confederacy had a lot of will and determination that the Union would not take over their homes and force them to do what they didn't want. The South also had some superior leaders, including General Robert E. Lee, Stonewall Jackson and J.E.B. Stuart. For many years, it looked like the South might win the war, especially when they tried to invade the North at Antietam and Gettysburg. Still, the North's greater number of men and more plentiful supplies finally won out and General Lee surrendered to General Grant in April 1865 at Appomatox Court House in Virginia. Several days later, a Southern actor shot and killed President Lincoln as he watched a play at Ford's Theater in Washington, DC.

Use an encyclopedia, the internet or an American history textbook to find out these answers to questions on the Civil War.

HISTORY

Although the firing on Fort Sumter is the official beginning of the Civil War, there were many things that led up to this outbreak. Find out what happened in Harper's Ferry, Virginia (now it is West Virginia) in 1859. Who is John Brown? How do you think this incident affected the start of the Civil War?

Look up these famous Civil War characters in your encyclopedia or on the internet and tell why they were important:
* Abraham Lincoln
*Edward Staunton
*Clara Barton
*Robert E. Lee
*Jefferson Davis
*Ulysses S. Grant
*George McClelland
*Stonewall Jackson
*John Wilkes Booth
*J.E.B. Stuart

Many battles were fought during the four years. Some of them were several days long and others were just brief skirmishes between the Union and Confederate armies. Look up these battles and see if you can find out their importance and which army was more victorious:
*First Battle of Bull Run (First Manassas)
*Battle of Antietam
*Battle of Fredericksburg

*Battle of Chancellorsville
*Battle of Gettysburg
*Battle of Cold Harbor
*Siege of Vicksburg
*Battle of Atlanta

Read another book about the American Civil War or visit a battlefield site near your home, if one is nearby. What do you think about the causes each side fought for? Which cause seems more just to you?

Find out about these important terms of the Civil War. What are they and why are they important?
*Emancipation Proclamation
*Gettysburg Address
*Appomatox Courthouse
*Copperhead
*Abolitionist

GEOGRAPHY

On a map of the United States, color the Northern states blue and the Southern states light brown (butternut). Remember that the western part of the US was mostly unsettled. The Northern states (The Union) were: Maine, Vermont, New Hampshire, Massachusetts, Connecticut, Rhode Island, New York, Pennsylvania, New Jersey, Delaware, Maryland, Ohio, Michigan, Kentucky, Indiana, Illinois, Wisconsin, Minnesota, Missouri, Nebraska, Kansas, and states to the west. The Southern states (Confederacy) were: Virginia, North Carolina, South Carolina, Georgia, Florida, Tennessee, Alabama, Mississippi, Louisiana, Arkansas and Texas.

Mark on your map the places where the above named battles took place. Also mark the capital of the Union: Washington, DC, and the capital of the

Confederacy: Richmond, Virginia. How far apart are these two capitals? Which do you think would be easier to defend? In which two of the above named battles happened on Union soil when the Confederacy tried to invade the Northern states?

Willy travels from Trenton, Michigan (just south of Detroit) to Fredericksburg, Virginia. How far did he go? What cities might he have passed through?

Willy then went by boat from Fredericksburg, Virginia to Hampton Roads, Virginia. Find Hampton Roads on the map. This is deep in Confederate Territory, but it was a Union held fort. Why do you think this fort was so important to the Union? What is the name of the bay on which Fortress Monroe sits? What is the name of the river that runs from this bay to the Union Capital, Washington, DC?

SCIENCE

The Civil War was known as a time of some of the greatest inventions of our time. Find out about these "firsts," how they were used in the war and why they were important.
    *hot air balloon
    *submarine
    *iron-clad ships
    *gatling gun
    *telegraph
    *land mines
    *flame throwers

Medical science has come a long way since the time of the Civil War. When a soldier was wounded in the arm or the leg, the bone was typically shattered. The doctors at the time didn't know how to fix the limb, so they cut it off so it wouldn't get infected and kill the man. Find out about how germs enter the body and can cause an infection. How do doctors treat an injury like a gunshot wound now?

Find out how a pontoon bridge is made. Where did they use pontoons in this story? Can you find out the history of the pontoon and where else in the Civil War they used pontoon bridges? Try to make your own pontoon bridge.

MUSIC

Each Civil War regiment had its own musicians. The musicians helped keep time while the regiment marched and kept up the spirits of the soldiers. The bugle in particular was used in rousing the men in the morning, sounding battle commands and lulling the men to sleep at night. Many times the musicians were young boys, like Willy in our story, who dreamed of being in battle. What else can you find out about musicians in the Civil War?

The songs of the Civil War are still around today. Look up these Civil War songs and find out something about them:

*John Brown's Body
*Battle Hymn of the Republic
*Dixie
*When Johnny Comes Marching Home Again
*Goober Peas
*Hail, Columbia
*Taps

If you play an instrument, try to learn a Civil War song. If not, learn to sing one.

ART

The Civil War was the first widespread use of a new art form: photography. James Brady was the most famous Civil War photographer. Early photography was a very time-consuming and expensive craft. Learn about photography in the Civil War and answer these questions:

1. Why were all the pictures in black and white?
2. What kind of equipment did they use to take pictures and develop them?
3. Why was photography so important during the Civil War?
4. How did they show battles and portraits of people before photography?
5. How is photography different today?
6. How is it the same?
7. What is the difference between film photography and digital photography?

VOCABULARY AND READING COMPREHENSION

Find five words from the story that you didn't know before reading *Willy Finds Victory*. Look up the meanings of the words in the dictionary. Write a sentence using each of the words you've just learned.

See if you can figure out the answers to these questions from the story.

1. What was the purpose of Willy's journey?
2. Where did Willy come from and where was he going?
3. Which war was being fought during the time of the story?
4. Who was Willy's constant companion?

5. Who were the people who helped Willy along the way and how did they help him?
6. Who was the man in the hospital and why did Willy go to see him?
7. Why was meeting Father Seelos important to Willy?
8. Why was Father Seelos at the hospital?
9. Where did Willy finally find his brother-in-law, Bill Smith?
10. What happened to Willy after he met his brother-in-law?
11. How did Willy meet Father Seelos again?
12. What was Willy's Victory?

RELIGION

Father Seelos talks to the soldiers about faith, hope and love, the theological virtues. Do you remember which was the great gift of all? Look up 1 Corinthians 13:4-7. What does St. Paul say about the virtue of love?

Father Seelos also talked about loving the enemy. Can you find where in the Bible Jesus talked about loving one's enemy? (Mt. 5:44; Lk. 10:27-37; Catechism of the Catholic Church 1825)

Willy portrays a number of other virtues in this story. Study the section in the Catechism of the Catholic Church (CCC) on virtues. (#1833-1845) Can you answer these questions?

1. What is a virtue?
2. What are the cardinal virtues?
3. What are the theological virtues?
4. List some virtues that Willy showed and give examples from the story of how he practiced these virtues.

5. Make a list of how Willy inspires you to practice virtues.

6. Father Seelos was known for his cheerfulness. His favorite virtue was charity. List some ways from the story that he practiced this virtue.

Do you know how to say the Rosary? If not, learn the prayers and plan to say at least one decade a day.

What other prayers do you say regularly? Try to learn a new one once a week and say it regularly.

At the end of the story, Willy's uncle softens a bit toward the Catholic faith. What did Willy and his sister do or say to win him over? What can you do to bring people closer to Jesus?

About the Author

Joan Stromberg lives just outside Louisville, KY with her husband of more than 30 years, Bob, and the six of their ten children who still live at home. The Strombergs have always home-schooled their children. As a young girl, Joan fell in love with history through reading historical fiction. Her dream was to be able to bring the love of history to children through writing historical fiction when she grew up. Combining her love of history with her love of the Catholic Church, the first books in the *Glory of America Series* were born.

About the Illustrator

Eileen McCook lives with her husband Terry and three daughters on the west coast of Florida. She has been homeschooling her children for over ten years. Eileen uses her extraordinary talents not only for book illustrations, but also as an art instructor and portrait painter. Her illustrations have thrilled readers of the Glory of America series for years.

About the Publisher

The goal of Behold Publications is to bring children to behold Christ through fun, interesting, educational, high quality products and to form apostles for the third millennium.